Angie

The Secret of Hillcrest House

Some secrets

Melanie Robertson-King

can be deadly!

Melanie

King Park Press

10.21.17

Published by King Park Press

House image: Melanie Robertson-King

Cloudy Sky & Moon: Shutterstock

Cover design: Julie Jordan

ISBN: 978-0-9921423-6-0

DEDICATION

For Don whose unwavering support means more to me than he will ever know. You’ve been there with encouragement during those periods of self-doubt and to celebrate my successes. Thank you.

ACKNOWLEDGMENTS

I want to thank Julie Jordan for the fantastic cover design she created with my image.

Thanks to everyone who entered my title contest. I ended up with 109 entries to choose from. It was difficult, but in the end, chosen in the order received, is the title you see on the book today – The Secret of Hillcrest House. Thank you, Greta Krasteva.

A special thank you to Chris Longmuir. You've helped me along the way, answering my questions (the same ones multiple times, no doubt), and making sure I didn't give up on myself. Your understanding and encouragement mean a lot to me.

And finally thank you to my team of beta readers without whose input this book wouldn't be what it is today. Take a bow, ladies – Dayna Leigh Cheser, Dorothy Bush, Kathy Throop, and Lynn L. Clark.

1

Jessica leaned forward in the driver's seat as she eased her Chevy Aveo around the corner on the crest of the hill. Not only was it a blind summit, but a blind summit on a curve. Once moving straight again, she glanced down to the passenger seat. The picture of the house – her house – she'd printed before leaving home lay there. A cursory glance at the GPS showed she was within a block of her new-to-her home.

Long before the mansion came on the market, every time Jessica had a pen or pencil in her hand, she sketched a house. From where had the idea for such a grand building originated? She had never seen a house similar to it before. It came straight from the pages of a fairy tale. Why did this place hold such fascination? There were no homes like it in Terra Cotta where she grew up. Even when she moved to Toronto to pursue her dream career as a graphic artist she'd not seen anything like it. Where was this magnificent structure?

From the time she first saw the real estate listing for Hillcrest House on the Internet, she knew she had to have it. Some inexplicable force within her compelled her to create images of it. Sight unseen, her sketches were identical to the mansion. She submitted an offer, never expecting them to accept it. When it was, an ecstatic Jessica began winding down her business in readiness for the move. The entire transaction took place online via websites, emails, scans and e-transfers.

She knew the house would be on her right so she slowed to a crawl and watched out the passenger window.

"You have reached your destination," the female voice with a British accent said.

Engrossed in looking for her new home, the noise startled her causing her to jump.

When Jessica set up the GPS unit, she chose a woman's voice over a man's. She'd never taken orders from a man before and wasn't about to start now. Besides, this voice was the least abrasive of the available selections.

Flipping on her right signal light, she pulled her car over to the curb and shut off the engine. Climbing out from behind the wheel, Jessica stretched. It had taken her about five hours to get here and her body knew it. She ran her fingers through her short, auburn hair then turned and leaned on folded arms on the roof of the car.

The granite, Victorian mansion stood to one side of the lot. A wrought iron fence surrounded the property. Patches of bare metal showed through the aqua green roof. Weathered plywood replaced glass in some of the upper windows. Others had gaping holes in the panes. Stained glass filled the round top upper frames. She hoped they were all intact. It would be next to impossible to replace them.

Paint peeled from the pillars and balusters of the sweeping verandah. Sections of the railing were missing. This once elegant home had fallen into a serious state of disrepair.

The blip of a siren startled her. She whipped around in time to see a police cruiser come to a stop behind her car. The officer emerged donning his Stetson as he approached. He was well over six feet tall and fit. Why did she have to notice his physique? She swore off men when her marriage fell apart. Now she was ogling a cop. She needed to get a grip.

"You can't park here. Didn't you see the *no parking* signs?" He pointed to one near her car.

"No. Sorry, I didn't."

"Pull around the corner and park on the far side of the street."

Jessica climbed back into her little Chevy. She didn't intend on taking orders from a man but this one wore a uniform and carried a gun. She drove around the corner and pulled into the driveway. A chain stretched between two stone pillars prevented her from going any further.

Parked on the property, there would be no reason for the cop to hang around. Still, when she exited her vehicle, the revealing brilliant white, perfect teeth. “And you are?”

“J-Jessica Maitland.”

“There was no one anywhere in the house. I’ve checked it from top to bottom.”

“But …,” she sagged against his shoulder.

How could that be? She saw the face in the window and the hands pressed against the glass. If no one had been inside the house, how did that rose get there? It was fresh. Not wilted. It made no sense. Her mind had to be playing tricks on her. Tired from the long drive and concentrating on the GPS directions, all she wanted was sleep.

2

“Have you got a place to stay tonight?” Alain asked. “You can’t stay here. That’s pretty obvious.”

“Cliffside Guest House.”

“Well, let’s get what you need out of your car and lock it up. I’ll drive you over there. It’s not far. Besides, you’re not in any state to get behind the wheel.” He stood and brushed off the seat of his trousers before extending his hand to help her to her feet.

Her shoulders slumped. She trudged ahead of him staring at the windows. Gone was the five foot nothing, redheaded fireball he encountered on his arrival.

When they reached her car, Alain noticed the contents of her handbag strewn over the interior. “You didn’t leave things like this when you followed me into the house, did you?”

“No,” she snapped at him. “Everything was as it should be and my purse was on the driver’s seat.”

“And you didn’t think to lock the vehicle when you left it unattended?”

“Duh, you had my keys.”

“Right. Sorry. I should file a report in case you discover something missing.”

“Don’t bother,” Jessica mumbled as she shoved things back into her handbag.

Alain felt guilty over the turn of events. He knew he was to blame for the ransacking of her car … well at least her purse. He started picking items up off the floor and handing them to Jessica. He froze when he reached again. His hand almost touched a selection of tampons in neon coloured wrappers. “I’ll let you get these,” he said feeling his cheeks heat up. Growing up with five sisters, he knew all too well, what these things were. Why was he embarrassed in front of a woman he'd met only a short time ago? Okay, she was an infuriating woman but an attractive one. Didn't even come up to his shoulder when standing beside him. Still, there was something about her.

He moved aside when she came around the car to collect the last of her spilt purse contents.

"You know, you don't have to drive me to the guesthouse. I can do it myself," she stated, ramming things into her handbag.

She stood and slammed the door shut, slinging her bag over her shoulder.

He smiled seeing her spunk returning. When she glared at him with her blue-green eyes, he changed his expression.

Jessica raised the hatch and pulled a black leather holdall towards her.

Alain reached for it. "This all you need?"

"Yes, but I want to make sure my camera and laptop are still in it." She unzipped the carry-on and rooted through the contents. "There's the laptop," she said pulling it out and sitting it on the car floor beside the bag. "And the camera."

Once Jessica had returned the items to the travel bag, Alain took it. He closed the hatch and locked the car. "Come on." He put his free hand behind her back steering her in the direction of his cruiser. Opening the back door, he put her bag on the seat.

"Do I have to ride back here, too?" she asked.

"No. You've not done anything wrong." He opened the front passenger door for her. The puzzled expression on her face said she'd never been in a police car before. Maybe she was unaccustomed to a man opening doors for her. Alain waited for her to settle in and fasten her seatbelt. Once she had, he rounded the car and slid behind the wheel. "You better have these," he said handing Jessica her car and house keys.

"Thanks."

Alain radioed his dispatch and brought them up to speed on the situation. He notified them he was taking Ms. Maitland to the Cliffside Guest House. He turned the key and the Crown Victoria roared to life. Checking the mirrors, he pulled a U-turn on the street and drove to the main road.

3

"Why, what brings you here, Constable Fournier?" Mrs. Bell greeted. The front door stood open a mere crack.

The woman looked to be in her mid to late sixties although it was hard to tell. Her white hair said older, but the lack of wrinkles said younger. Jessica hoped when she reached the woman's age, she remained as attractive.

"This is Ms. … Jessica Maitland. She's the new owner of Hillcrest House. I believe she's staying here tonight," he replied.

"Yes, she is." The woman opened the door wide and invited them into the foyer. "Set your bag over there, dear," she said gesturing to a place on the floor beneath an antique wall clock. "I'll show you around then we'll get you settled in your room. I just made a fresh pot of coffee. Can you stay for a cup, constable?"

"As tempting an offer as it is Mrs. B, I've got to get back to work. By the way, she fainted earlier." He turned to Jessica. "If you need anything Jess … I mean Ms. Maitland, give us a call."

"I-I will." Jessica watched Alain leave wishing he could stay. Why could she not get him out of her mind? Sure, he was good looking and she could get lost in those blue eyes. But she was behaving like a lovesick teenager in the throes of her first crush.

"Come along, dear, we'll have a natter over a cup."

Lost in her daydream about the handsome police constable, Jessica jumped.

"I'm sorry. I didn't mean to startle you." Mrs. Bell put her arm around Jessica's shoulders and led her through the downstairs. "In here is the living room. You're welcome to use it any time. Satellite TV although there is a set in your room if you prefer to use it."

"Do you have Wi-Fi? I didn't see anything about it when I made the booking."

"Yes. I don't know what I'd do without the Internet. My children and grandchildren live far away now and don't get home often. It's an easy way of keeping in touch."

Arthritis-gnarled hands held a newspaper in the corner of the room. A pair of legs protruded below it. Jessica hoped there was a body attached to the limbs.

"Bill, this is Jessica Maitland."

He lowered his paper, grunted a response and went back to reading. During the brief time he was visible, Jessica noticed he hadn't aged as well as his wife. Either that, or he was quite a bit older than Mrs. Bell.

The tour continued with the dining room, where she would have breakfast. A small powder room occupied what at one time might have been a closet. It wasn't much bigger than that.

The living and dining rooms were dark and filled with heavy, formal furnishings. The kitchen was a complete contrast to them. It was bright and airy with gleaming white, Shaker style cabinets. Black, granite counter tops and stainless steel appliances completed the country kitchen look. A white and woodgrain round pedestal table with matching chairs stood in the middle of the room.

"Sit down, dear," Mrs. Bell said as she flitted through the kitchen.

A few moments later, a mug of steaming coffee appeared on the table along with cream, sugar and a plate of cookies.

"I like my guests to feel welcome," she said taking a seat opposite Jessica. "Help yourself."

For a few minutes, they drank their coffee in amiable silence. This was the first decent cup Jessica had that didn't come from a Keurig. That was one of her better purchases.

"Are you married, dear?"

The question caught Jessica off guard. She choked and spluttered cookie crumbs onto the table. "N-no," she stammered.

"Just as well with the way you were looking at Constable Fournier. He's a lovely young man. So tragic about his wife, though."

Alain married? Her heart sank. She hadn't seen a wedding ring on his finger. Mind you, that didn't mean much. Her father never wore a ring of any kind and her ex had his wedding ring off more than on. Tragic? Mrs. Bell's last sentence finally permeated Jessica's tired mind. "What about his wife?"

"The poor thing. Lovely person she was."

Was as in past tense. Had something happened to her? If so, what? Could she ask without appearing nosey? Mrs. Bell spared her the embarrassment.

"A drunk driver hit her coming home from work one night. She was an emergency room nurse, you see. Constable Fournier got the call. The police didn't know it was his wife until later. Otherwise, they would have sent another officer to the scene. Mangled her leg something terrible and the poor thing ended up losing it. Anyway, she couldn't live with her disability. She threw herself over the cliff the spring after it happened when Angel Falls was at its peak."

"How long ago?"

"Two years next spring."

At that moment, all Jessica wanted was to find Alain and make his hurt go away. "Did they have children?"

"No."

That was one small mercy. Tears pricked at the backs of Jessica's eyes. Overwhelmed with grief for this man she hardly knew. Her feelings of inadequacy rose to the surface. Had she been a better mother. Had she gone in and checked on her infant daughter sooner. Maybe her child would still be alive. Maybe her husband wouldn't have slept his way through the office tower where he worked. She breathed in and held it before exhaling hoping she could regain her composure.

"Whatever possessed you to buy Hillcrest House of all places?"

"I was looking for a fresh start. Angel Falls seemed far enough away to give me that." Jessica didn't dare tell Mrs. Bell, a complete stranger, about the sketches she'd done of a house identical to Hillcrest House long before seeing it. "I started looking at houses on the Internet and fell in love with it as soon as I saw it," she sighed before continuing. "The pictures online look nothing like the house I saw earlier today. I don't know how old they are but … the place is a dump now. It's going to take forever and a small fortune to get it fixed up and livable." The tears she suppressed earlier flowed and she had no way to stem the tide.

Mrs. Bell rushed around the table and tried to comfort her but it was to no avail. The more she tried, the more Jessica wailed.

"What's going on in here?" Bill asked. "A body can't even read their newspaper with all this racket going on."

"Hush you. Can't you see the poor girl is upset?" She produced a tissue and handed it to Jessica. "She's just found out that the house she bought here in Angel Falls needs more work than she thought it would."

A few ragged breaths and Jessica regained her control.

"She do something daft like buy Hillcrest?"

More tears flowed. If she had known the house was in such a state of disrepair. If. That two-letter word held huge importance. She would have walked away rather than go through with it. The photos showed a clean, empty house. Rich wooden wainscoting, shiny hardwood floors, and sparkling chandeliers completed the look.

"You're not helping, Bill. Get your coffee and leave me to it."

Mug in hand, he shuffled out of the room shaking his head as he went.

"Wh-why did he say that?" Jessica stammered. She wiped her eyes with the tissue and blew her nose.

"There are rumours about the old place. Not that I put much stock in them."

"What kind?"

"It's haunted so they say." Mrs. Bell brought the carafe to the table and warmed their coffees.

"I can see where that idea would come from," Jessica replied.

"There's been such a turnover of owners these last years. People buy. Start renovations and before you know it; the place is back on the market again. It used to be such a pretty house."

"And it will be again," Jessica said with confidence. Too bad, she didn't feel it.

A clock chimed from the front of the house. "Oh my, is that the time? I have to get supper started. I don't feed guests evening meals but since it's just you. I hope you like Tourtiere and Caesar salad."

"That sounds lovely."

"I'll show you to your room. You can freshen up, relax and I'll come get you when it's ready."

4

Mrs. Bell opened the door to an upstairs room above the kitchen. "Here you are. Your en-suite is through there, plenty of closet space and feel free to put your things in the dresser."

After the woman left, Jessica fell backwards onto the four-poster bed. Peace and quiet at last. Mrs. Bell was an angel but man oh man, could she talk. Maybe that's why her husband didn't say much – he couldn't get a word in edgewise.

If she stayed lying down much longer, she would be asleep. Forcing herself off the bed, she grabbed her holdall. Jessica unpacked her camera, laptop and toiletries. She pushed the en-suite door open. The size of the bathroom amazed her. An enormous soaker tub and separate shower stall were along the far wall. The toilet and sink nestled along either side of the door.

She placed her laptop on the small dressing table. Network and password information keyed in, Jessica logged into her browser. She searched for Angel Falls. Besides a map on the right side of the screen, the top result was a Wikipedia entry. She clicked on it. The information focused on the village. Further down the page she discovered details about the falls themselves. *An underground stream running beneath Richard Street feeds the falls. Over centuries, they formed through crevices in the limestone cliff adjacent to Royal Avenue. After the spring thaw, the falls are at their peak. Indian legend says the mist rising during this time takes the shape of an angel.*

It was mid-June. The falls would not flow, this time of year. The water would only escape in a trickle. The leafed out trees obliterated the view from below the cliff.

Recalling Mrs. Bell's story about Alain's wife, Jessica opened another tab in her browser. She searched for suicide at

Angel Falls. A myriad of results appeared. Before she had the opportunity to look closer, the call to supper followed a soft knock on her door. Not wanting to lose the results, Jessica set the screen saver to blank after a minute. “Coming,” she responded.

***

“Thanks, Mrs. Bell. This is so generous feeding me supper when you don’t do it for other guests.”

“It’s quite all right, dear. And please call me Eunice.” She reached over and patted the back of Jessica’s hand. “So where do you want to start.”

“Start?”

“You know – with your renovations.”

“Before I can do anything, even think of doing anything, I need to get a glazier in to repair the windows. I’d like to get low-e, triple glazed ones installed. With the number of them in the place, I wouldn’t be able to do anything else.”

“Bill, who did our windows here?” Eunice asked.

“Oh, that was … whatshisname … I’ve got his card here somewhere. I’ll look it up and give it to you, Miss Maitland.”

“Please call me Jessica,” she replied smiling. “And I need a reputable locksmith. When I stopped at the house earlier, there was someone inside.”

“Oh?” Mrs. Bell put her fork down. “What room did you see them in?”

“The room over the side porch.”

The colour drained from the woman’s face. Right, Eunice didn’t put much stock in the Hillcrest House gossip.

“Alain … Constable Fournier … searched the house from top to bottom. There wasn’t anyone inside. When I followed him, I found a long-stemmed, red rose on the back of a couch in one of the downstairs rooms. It was fresh like it was just cut.”

Jessica was beginning to scare herself relaying the events from earlier that day. That meant there was some basis to the rumours. Did she want to share a Victorian mansion with a ghost? Or worse, a bevy of spirits? "If you'll excuse me, I'm exhausted after the long drive and everything. I'm going to have an early night. I'll see you both in the morning. If you could find that business card for the window guy before breakfast, I'd appreciate it."

Returning to her room, Jessica went straight to her computer. She continued where she had left off in her mission to find out more about Alain's dead wife. Photos of the woman accompanied the articles. She was beyond attractive. She was drop dead gorgeous with blue eyes, blonde hair, pert mouth and perfect teeth. Jessica felt inferior when compared to this woman. She was plain, short and had red hair that wasn't even an attractive shade.

When she saw the photo of Alain and his wife with the Eiffel Tower in the background, her feelings of inadequacy grew. Honeymoon? The couple looked so happy and in love with each other. All Jessica got was a single night in the Royal York in downtown Toronto. Still, it was a beautiful hotel but not her dream honeymoon destination. She should have known then that her marriage wouldn't last.

Beginning to yawn and having difficulty keeping her eyes open, Jessica shut down her computer. She couldn't believe she had been online that long. She collapsed on the bed, clutched a small throw pillow to her chest and thought about Alain. How did he cope? First with his wife's accident and losing her leg followed by her suicide? Would he want another relationship? Was he ready? Was she ready? She fell asleep seeing his fit body and smiling face.

5

The following morning, Jessica woke to the smell of frying bacon and strong coffee. She jumped out of bed, showered, applied makeup, and got dressed.

Downstairs, she headed straight for the kitchen. Jessica forgot Mrs. Bell served breakfast in the formal dining room. Directed to the other room by the woman, she discovered a list of tradespeople at her place at the table.

"Bill put this together for you last night, dear. The ones with stars are the folks we've dealt with although everyone on the list is reputable."

"Thank you both. I'm going to need an electrician, too. The wiring is old and even just having the electricity turned on isn't going to be enough. Unfortunately, I'm not going to be able to move in as soon as I'd hoped."

"Stay here as long as you need," Eunice replied and poured Jessica a cup of coffee.

"Thank you."

***

Jessica gathered her handbag, keys, cellphone and Canon DSLR. Armed with these and the list put together by Mr. Bell, she set off on foot to Hillcrest House. Having a place to stay was one less worry. Finding a place to store her belongings for the foreseeable future was something else. She hadn't noticed driving through the village yesterday if there were storage lockers. Still, she'd be able to find that out easily enough.

She had to walk past the cliff top where Angel Falls flowed. The metal guardrail along the side of the road showed its age. Dull and dented, paint scraped from car bumpers. At least it prevented vehicles from leaving the road. Jessica stopped and peered down over the precipice. Thinking she saw a trickle of water, she leaned forward for a closer look. Her left foot slid and she gripped the barrier to keep from tumbling to the ground below. Was that what happened to Alain's wife? Did she lose her footing and fall? Or did she kill herself?

Once she reached Hillcrest House, Jessica pulled out the list and started making phone calls. Luckily, the glazier and locksmith could come right away. The electrician wouldn't be able to until the following day.

The front verandah creaked and groaned under her feet. She would have to replace the boards before long – before someone fell through them. Letting herself in the front door, she left it wide open to let in the available light.

She took her camera out of her handbag and took photos of the foyer, the corridor leading to the kitchen, and the stairs. Next, Jessica entered the large sitting room off to the right. Closed shutters covered many of the windows. She worked her way around opening them to let in what light could penetrate the filthy glass. More photos from every angle in the room. An enormous fireplace with a huge mantle mirror above it stood along the inside wall next to the doorway. Cobwebs covered it like every other ornate surface in the room. Window trim, the chandelier, and table lamps wore a coating of the gossamer fibers. Mounted on either side of the firebox were two demonic heads with rings in their mouths. Jessica had never seen anything like them before. Their evil appearance was further emphasized by the sticky webbing stretching down from the mirror. She took about a dozen photographs of just the heads. Across from the hearth, a section of the wainscoting at least ten feet wide reached all the way to the ceiling. In the rest of the room, it stopped about three feet lower.

Over the next few hours, Jessica visited every room in the house taking photos as she went. When she reached the room where she'd seen the person in the window the day before it was much colder than the others. An icy, clammy chill came over her. Sweat beaded and ran down the back of her neck, settling at the waistband of her jeans. She shivered but carried on.

"Art Smith, here."

Jessica's heart leapt into her throat. She whipped around. "You scared the life out of me. What were you thinking?"

"I hollered from the front door but I guess you didn't hear me. I'm sorry."

"And you are?"

"You wanted a quote on getting your windows fixed."

"Sorry, not thinking straight."

Jessica left the man to measure windows so he could come up with a quote. She continued taking photographs on the second level. The room below the turret had a floor to ceiling bow window and a door in the side of it leading to a balcony. Not knowing what state its wooden floor was in, she didn't venture outside onto it. The boards in the side porch and main entrance verandah were in rough condition. She did not fancy falling through on this level.

A small staircase led up to the attic rooms. With the slopes of the roof and turret, headroom along the outside walls was at a premium. When she took pictures from this side of the room, the low ceilings forced her to crouch. She bumped her head a few times when she straightened up.

While in the corridor that linked the rooms on this level, Jessica attempted to open a door but found it locked. There were a number of skeleton keys on her ring so she tried each one in turn, but none would unlock it. She made a mental note to have the locksmith either fix the mechanism or replace it. Wherever this door led couldn't be a closet. Those doors all opened with little effort. This one had to lead to something else – maybe a secret passage.

"Oh miss, that's me away," Art called up from the landing below.

Jessica met him at the top of the stairs to the second level. At least the windows up in the attic rooms were still intact. "I'll see you out." Jessica went down to meet him.

"I'll get the quote done up and to you in the next couple of days. Where can I send it?"

"Can you email it? That would be best."

"Certainly."

"Great. It's Jess Maitland – all one word and no caps – at gmail dot com. Or, I'm staying with the Bells at Cliffside Guest House; you could drop a hard copy off there."

"Ah, I know them well. I'll drop the quote by. They're good people, they are."

Jessica knew that already. They'd taken her in and treated her like a member of the family – Mrs. Bell especially.

"This peeling paint could be an issue," Art continued. "Depending on how long ago the place was last painted, I'm guessing the stuff they used was lead based."

Jessica's heart sank. That meant having someone who specialized in removing it come and do the job. Her remodelling budget had taken blow after blow. She pulled out her cell phone and called Mr. Bell. "Hi Bill, it's Jessica. I hate to bother you but I need someone who knows what they're doing to come in and remove lead paint from the house. All the rooms on the second floor are in a terrible state. I think it's because this is where the majority of the broken windows are. And my luck, there's asbestos in the house, too, that I'll have to get removed."

"I'll ask around. In the meantime, you shouldn't be spending any more time in that place."

Those were the last words she wanted to hear. The work on the house would come to a halt with this unexpected turn of events. One step forward, ten steps back. Why had she been so quick to sign on the dotted line in the first place? She should have had a home inspection done first. At least then, she'd have known what she was up against and made an informed decision. But no, she had to jump in with both feet and suffer the consequences later. It wasn't the first time she'd done this. Damn it. Why couldn't she have inherited the logic her father possessed? No, she got all the emotional genes.

***

The shrill ring of the twist bell on the front door echoed through the corridors. When they reached the front door, she was still chatting with the glazier about the Bells and Angel Falls.

"You must be the locksmith?" She hoped so and not just someone off the street wanting to get their jollies by looking inside the house.

"Yes. Wilfred Jones."

"Afternoon Wilf. How are things?" Art inquired.

"Well, you know. Can't complain. And you?"

"About the same." Mr. Smith nodded to her and started out the front door.

Jessica walked him down the steps and to the end of the verandah on the driveway side of the house. As she waved him off, he looked back over his shoulder but not at her. His gaze held at a spot on the second floor. He then picked up his pace almost as if he saw something in one of the upper windows. Had he seen the same person she saw in the room over the kitchen the day before? Or maybe even someone else in another part of the house? At times, the place gave Jessica the creeps but her love for the mansion far outweighed its scariness.

She turned her attention back to the man in front of her. "I'll show you the doors that need new locks. There's the double front door here. There are two off the kitchen at the back," she stated leading the way. "There's one upstairs in the room below the turret that goes out to a balcony. I'd like to have deadbolts installed in them."

"Excellent decision. Time was, a skeleton key and lock were enough to safeguard your property. Unfortunately, those days are long gone," he replied. "That won't be a huge job to do. Are you sure the wood isn't rotten? Don't want to start drilling openings and find punky wood or worse – termites. The hardware that's on the door looks to be in good enough shape so we won't replace it."

That would be a saving not to mention something going right.

"Wait, there's another door up on the top level. I've tried all my keys and none of them worked. Would you mind having a look?"

"I'm here now. Might as well. Save you paying for another call."

Jessica led the way up to the attic. When she turned the corner at the top of the stairs, she gasped. The door she couldn't open earlier stood ajar. "I-I don't understand," she stammered. "This door wouldn't budge earlier."

The locksmith stepped forward, opened and closed the door a dozen or so times with no problem. "Are you sure this is the right door?"

"Yes, I'm sure." She tiptoed closer. Behind the door was a narrow, steep stairway. A beam of light shone down from the top. It was no secret passage but where did the steps lead? And where was the light coming from?

"This place has a widow's walk on the roof?" Wilf asked.

"Yes."

"This is likely the stairs to it. The hatch at the top isn't closed tight, is my best guess, and that's why we can see light. I'll go up and close it. You don't want rain or snow getting in and rotting the stairs out." The man pulled a small flashlight out of his pocket and climbed. The treads creaked with each step he took.

Curious to see what it was like up there, Jessica followed him.

"This should have a lock on the inside," he mused. "Even just a good heavy padlock. It would take a lot for someone to get to the roof. If the hatch isn't secured from inside, it would be easy to get in and down into the house."

"Will you look after it, too?"

"Yup." He pushed on the hatch but it didn't budge. "Rusted hinges, I'll bet." Trying again, he put even more weight behind it and with a deafening screech of metal on metal, the door opened.

"Can I see?

The tradesman stepped aside so Jessica could climb further. When she was out of the narrow opening from her head to her waist, she pulled herself out the rest of the way. Standing on the roof of her house felt strange. The view from this vantage point was amazing. She could see for miles in every direction. Taking her time, she made her way around the edges, clinging to the railing. The space up here was even bigger than she imagined. It would be a great place to put a couple of chairs and a small table. She envisioned sitting at her bistro set watching the sunset with good company and a bottle of wine. As soon as that thought popped into her head, she thought of Alain. Would he like to watch the sun go down with her up here? Even though it was out in the open, it felt secluded. They could make love under the stars.

"I best get a move on," Wilf said, interrupting her fantasy.

"Yeah, sorry. Got caught up in the view." Her cheeks burned so she knew she was blushing. She climbed back inside and down the stairs.

Once she'd passed the locksmith, he pulled the hatch down and fastened it.

By now, Jessica stood by the door on the attic level of the house.

"Do you want a deadbolt put on this door, too, or leave it as is? Personally, I don't think it needs one as long as there's a good heavy lock up there." He nodded in the direction of the trap door at the head of the stairs.

"But why couldn't I unlock the door and then when we came upstairs it was wide open? And it opened and closed for you. I don't get it."

"Old houses. Could be just you moving about jarred it open. What finish do you want?"

"Finish?"

"Brass, antique brass – my personal favourite for a house of this age – or polished nickel?"

"I agree. The antique brass would fit best."

"I have a catalogue out in the van. I'll get it and give you a couple of days to look it over and decide which locks you want."

"Days? I want them installed now."

6

Jessica flipped through the catalogue the locksmith left with her. So many styles to choose from. But she didn't need the entire entry set. Just a deadbolt. Still, a couple of full handles with separate locks caught her eye. Why not splash out and order something fancy for the double front door? The house used to have great curb appeal and it would again. Time and money were the only prerequisites. Time she had. Money not so much.

Alone in the house now that the two tradesmen had left, Jessica walked to the kitchen. She opened the side door that led onto the porch facing the driveway. The hinges creaked in protest. WD40 would fix that and she made a mental note to buy some. One of the previous owners had installed a chain on the door so she fastened it before checking the other one. She could get away with just deadbolts on these two doors. A bit of savings here. The ones for this room wouldn't have to be elaborate. She went upstairs and checked the balcony door. Jessica decided it should have a full lockset like the front door below. After all, it almost faced the street so it should have the full treatment like the main entrance. The only other door she wanted a deadbolt on was the one on the stairs to the widow's walk. And if possible, one keyed from either side.

***

When Jessica walked from the front door to her car, a huge crow slid down the mansion's metal roof. Its claws screeched like chalk on a blackboard. She cringed. Covered in lustrous, black plumage, a lone white feather stuck out from the side of its neck. It cawed and squawked, bobbing its head up and down. The sound got louder and louder as more and more crows arrived. Their cacophony was deafening. One of the incoming birds swooped past Jessica. It flew close enough that she felt its wingtips graze her head. It swept to the railing of the widow's walk – now black with the raucous creatures.

Frightened, she struggled to get her thumb onto the unlock button of her key fob. When she succeeded, she pushed it and dove into her car, locking it behind her with all the windows wound up.

The crow with the white feather flew down from the roof and landed on the hood. She screamed and hit the horn but it did nothing to dissuade the creature. Instead, it walked to the windshield and started tugging at the wiper blades.

Shaking, when Jessica tried to put the key in the ignition, she dropped the ring onto the floor. She reached down to retrieve it without taking her eyes off her feathered nemesis. Still more crows flew in. Besides the birds on the railing, they lined up along the eaves of the house. More perched on the overhead hydro wires.

When she got the car started, Jessica threw it in reverse. She gunned the engine, almost losing control as she backed out of the driveway. Where had they all come from? She had never seen so many crows in one place in her life. There were too many to count. A real-life episode of *The Birds* played out in front of her.

The sooner she got away from here, the happier she would be. After she turned right onto Royal Avenue, the moving van crested the hill in her rear view mirror. She would have to return to the house and those birds.

Jessica pulled her car over and waited for the truck to turn onto Richard Street. When it did, she used someone's driveway to turn around and drove back to Hillcrest House. Peering out the car windows before exiting, she saw that the crows were gone. They had disappeared as fast as they appeared. Creepy.

"Where do you want your furniture?" one of the burly movers asked.

Closing the door, she approached the men. "You can't leave it here. The house isn't ready. It needs to go into storage. Do you know if there are any places in the area?"

"There was one about fifty miles back. But there aren't many big enough for this lot."

Dejected, Jessica leaned against the box of the moving van. "Now what am I going to do? The house is so far from being move-in ready."

"Not our problem, lady. You paid us to deliver and we've delivered."

Her white knight in the form of one police officer drove by the house and pulled across the front of the truck.

"What seems to be the problem?" he asked approaching the men.

"She won't let us unload the truck and take her junk – I mean belongings – into the house."

"Alain, you know the state of the place. I've got enough to contend with getting it move-in ready with everything the previous owners left behind."

He strode closer and took Jessica aside. "Are you sure you can't store everything in the truck in one room? I'm willing to help you make space for it."

Jessica shook her head. "I'm not leaving any of my stuff here before I have the new locks installed at the least. Truth is, I need to get the house cleaned and decorated before anything gets brought in. What am I going to do?"

Alain scratched his head. "Call the Bells. Bill must know someone willing to let you store your things in their barn or something."

"Okay. But aren't barns usually infested with mice?"

"Not always. I grew up on a farm. We had plenty of cats to keep the mouse population under control."

Shoulders sagging, Jessica returned to her car. She pulled her phone out of her handbag and phoned Eunice. Sobbing, she related her problem with not having a place to store her things.

"It's only until you have the house cleaned and the old furniture removed, dear?"

"Y-yes."

"We have a couple of outbuildings that you can use. You'll be staying with us until then so it's settled."

Breathing a sigh of relief, Jessica thanked the woman. The Bells were too good to be true. They'd extended her stay no questions asked and now she could store her things there. "I'll send the movers now." She disconnected the call and turned to Alain. "Thank you," she mouthed.

7

When Jessica returned to the guesthouse two hours later, Eunice and another woman chatted at the kitchen table over coffee. "Will you join us, dear?"

"I don't want to interrupt."

"Don't be silly. You look like you've had an awful day." Mrs. Bell leapt to her feet and poured Jessica a cup. "Come sit down. My, aren't those cute socks."

Jessica looked down at her white socks covered with multi-coloured polka-dots. "Thanks," she sighed as she sat. Eunice was right. It had been a day from hell.

"The movers brought your furniture. Bill directed traffic so to speak and has everything stored away out back. Your boxes of clothing and personal items are in your room."

"Where is your husband? I'd like to thank him."

"You'll have to wait until later. He's gone off for his afternoon constitutional. Picks up his newspaper and catches up on the gossip at the convenience store."

Jessica chuckled. She could picture the man doing just that.

"I expected you back when the men came with your things."

"I needed a break from the house, the movers – everything. I walked to the bottom of Angel Falls. Not much to see this time of year."

"Where are my manners?" Eunice changed the subject. "I've not introduced you two. Jessica, this is Marion. She lives just up the way. Marion, this is Jessica. She's the new owner of Hillcrest House and is staying here while she gets it into move-in condition."

Mrs. Bell's guest went ashen when she heard the name of

the house.

"If you don't mind, I'll take my coffee to my room. I want to download the photos I took at the house today onto my laptop. While I've got contractors in working, I can get ideas for decorating and what I want to use each room for."

"That's fine, dear. Off you go."

At times, Jessica felt like she was reporting to her mother the way Mrs. Bell behaved towards her. The woman's own children had moved away. It wasn't a stretch to think she'd act that way with people around that same age.

Jessica settled in at the dressing table with her camera and computer. Removing the SD card from the one device, she inserted it in the slot of the other. While the laptop booted up, she sipped her coffee.

The photographs looked creepier than the actual house did. The first few were of the rooms downstairs with the peeling paint, wall and ceiling paper, cobweb infested chandeliers, shutters and shades. She clicked through the images, making notes on a pad for the rooms they went with for possible paint colours and window treatments.

When the first picture of the bedroom over the kitchen appeared on the screen, a child-like apparition loomed. It hovered about six inches above the floor. She continued to the next photo of the room. It was in that one, too. And the next. Each time it was in a different corner. Spooked, Jessica slammed the laptop shut. Her heart pounded and she broke out into a cold sweat. She wrapped her cold, shaking hands around her hot mug of coffee to warm them and calm herself but it didn't work. She'd been alone in the house except when the tradesmen were there. She knew that.

Determined not to let the ghostlike figure get to her, Jessica opened her computer again. Viewing the remaining pictures, that was the only room where anything strange showed. She checked her camera. There weren't any marks on the lens but she cleaned it anyway. She removed it from the body, inspected the other end, and inside the device. The spectral shadow was unique to that room.

8

The following morning, Bill joined Jessica in the dining room. "I found the name of a company that removes lead paint. They're called Get the Lead Out. Brad Foster runs the place. I got his number here somewhere," he stated as he dug through the contents of his wallet. "Here it is." He held it out to her.

Jessica accepted the piece of paper. If the house contained lead paint, she'd have to get it removed, no doubt about that. But she didn't have the inclination to tackle a job of that magnitude. "Thanks, Bill. You're a star. I'll give him a call and arrange to meet him at the house. The sooner that job gets done and dusted, the sooner everything else can."

Finishing her breakfast, she toyed with the piece of paper. The name of the company was catchy and it said what they did, more or less. It could also refer to a plumbing company and replacing old water pipes. She tried to banish that thought from her mind. She'd poured enough good money after bad and still wasn't finished. The last thing she needed was to have to have the plumbing redone.

Jessica drank down the last of her coffee and returned to her room. She picked up her cell phone and discovered it was dead. So much for using it to set up an appointment. Would the Bells mind if she used their landline instead? It shouldn't be a problem if the call was local. If not, then she would have to wait until her phone charged.

***

She found Mrs. Bell in the kitchen. "Do you mind if I use your phone to call the lead paint guy? My cell phone is dead."

"Of course not. Use the one in the living room. Bill's gone

out so there's no one to disturb you."

"Thank you," Jessica called over her shoulder as she walked to the other room to make her call.

A man answered on the third ring. "Get the Lead Out, Brad here."

"I need to get a quote for having the lead paint removed from my house." She heard pages turning on the other end.

"I've got time free this afternoon. Say two-thirty?"

"That's fine." Jessica said, disappointed it wasn't earlier but at least it was the same day.

"What's the address?"

"Hillcrest House, Royal Avenue, Angel Falls."

"Oh."

She recognized the tone in his voice. Now that he knew where it was, he sounded uninterested in the job.

***

At least today, another two appointments with workmen would be out of the way. When she made the appointment with the electrician, he hadn't given her a time. She had no idea when he would arrive.

It was a gorgeous morning – sunny and warm so Jessica dressed in a pair of jean shorts and t-shirt, a pair of wool work socks, and her pink steel-toed boots. She could tackle some of the outdoor work. Grapevine and other trailing weeds, and umpteen dandelions took over the lawn.

Stone pillars at about eight foot intervals supported the verandah, its roof and the balcony above it. Using the bow rake she'd borrowed from the Bells, she started next to the house and worked towards the wrought iron fence at the sidewalk on Royal Avenue.

Before she got to the first footing, her arms ached from yanking vines and weeds, and pulling the tool through the long grass. Jessica paused, pushed her hair off her forehead with her arm, and removed the work gloves. As she flexed her fingers, she realized how red and blistered her hands were.

She walked to her Chevy Aveo and retrieved the first aid

kit. While she searched for something to cover her blisters, a lone crow glided on the thermals overhead. Leaning back against the car, Jessica watched it intrigued at the way it soared without having to expend much energy.

As the bird dropped lower in the sky, she noticed a white feather on the side of its neck in the same place as on the one that attacked her car. Without hesitation, Jessica bundled the medical supplies into the vehicle and locked it.

A white minivan with a Lightning Electrical logo emblazoned on it pulled into the driveway. Swallowing hard and taking a deep breath, she approached the vehicle as the driver exited.

His navy blue shirt had a lightning bolt on the badge above the pocket with his first name – Steve – embroidered below the company logo. "Hi, you're looking to have some electrical work done?"

"Follow me. Sorry, I must look a fright. Been doing yard work," she offered. Why did she say that? She didn't know the man. Why did she feel compelled to apologize to him straight away? After the house was re-wired, she'd likely never see him again. And that was if she hired him in the first place. "The whole house needs rewiring," she continued as she escorted him to the front door.

His moustache needed trimming. It covered his top lip and most of his upper teeth. She cringed. She wasn't a big fan of facial hair on a man. She much preferred men to be clean-shaven like Alain, although he went further and shaved his entire head.

***

Steve pulled a small flashlight out of his belt. He inspected the push button switch on the wall.

"I want to keep the chandeliers."

"That shouldn't be a problem." He walked through the huge room on the right side of the foyer. Steve shone his light around looking for receptacles and switches. He made notes and took measurements as he went. From there he moved to the sitting room and dining room on the opposite side of the hall.

When he walked around the kitchen, Steve mumbled. This was going to be an enormous job. Far bigger than any he'd bid on before. At least he assumed she had other firms quoting on it. "You're living here?" he asked raking his fingers through his wavy, light brown hair.

"Does it look like it?" she laughed. "I just got possession a couple of days ago and want to get the place fixed up before I do move in. I'm staying in a guesthouse nearby."

"Can you show me the rest of the place?" He smiled at her.

Jessica led the way up to the second floor. He left her sitting at the foot of the stairs leading to the next level while he continued his inspection.

"You ready to go up to the attic?" she asked when he emerged from the last room.

"Lead on. I've got to say, even in this state, this place is impressive," he whistled.

"There's another set of stairs this way. There's a light fixture on the wall behind the door. Nothing fancy, bare bulb and pull chain. I'd like it moved closer to the ceiling and a switch as close to the top of the stairs as you can get, and one here on this side at the bottom."

Steve tried the door and it opened. He peered inside and shone his flashlight up to the top. "Yup. That won't be a problem." After inspecting the rest of this level and taking more measurements, he closed his book. "The only thing I've not seen yet is the panel. Can you show me where it is?"

"I don't know."

"Huh?" He arched his eyebrow.

"I don't know where it is."

"Likely in the basement. That's usually where they're located."

"This is going to sound stupid, but I don't know how to get down there."

Steve shook his head and started down the stairs. He checked behind the door under the main staircase. "Thought for sure this would be where the steps would be. Usually, they're put one under the other," he commented emerging from what was a small closet.

"Maybe it's an outside entrance?"

"Could be. Never thought of that." He raked his hand through his hair again and went outside.

Something hadn't felt right to him in a couple of the second floor rooms but he couldn't put his finger on it. The one over the kitchen felt dark and dismal, despite the sunshine streaming in the windows. Sad. So was the bedroom that opened onto the balcony. He felt passion and rage in the other one on the front of the house. What it all added up to, he didn't know. All he knew was he was glad to be outdoors.

At the foot of the front verandah stairs, Steve turned right and worked his way around the house. When he pulled into the driveway, he hadn't seen anything that resembled an outside basement entrance. He wasn't looking then either.

Three quarters of the way around the house, he discovered the metal bulkhead; painted the same colour as the roof. "Found it. You want to see where it is?" he asked when he returned. He led the way past pieces of wood from broken latticework, railings and other debris along the side of the building next to the neighbouring property.

"You got the key? There's a padlock on it."

"I think so." She felt her pockets until she found them. "This it?" she asked, handing it to him.

He tried the key and the padlock opened. The door creaked when he lifted it. "You coming?"

"No. You're all right. I'll stay up here."

Steve turned his flashlight on and descended into the murky, musty cellar. He turned the light at each wall looking for the panel. As he cast the beam along the far side, a pair of red, glowing orbs appeared. At first, he thought it might have been a raccoon or other animal trapped down there. But they were too high off the floor for that. There wasn't anything for it to be on top of either. The only objects straight across the room were these flaming eyes and the stone foundation behind them.

It had to be his imagination. *Addams Family* type house, of course he'd start seeing things that weren't there. Wouldn't he?

It took a while but he found the panel, padlocked shut

sealing it. He knew it was the old type fuses and likely pennies behind some of them. It was a wonder the place never burned to the ground.

As he turned towards the bulkhead to leave, a low snarl sounded behind him sending chills down his spine. He scampered up the steps and outside.

Steve emerged from the cellar a few minutes later. “Don’t blame you for not wanting to go down there. But that’s where your panel is so the poor sucker that has to change it will get the honours.” He gasped trying to catch his breath.

9

A black Charger with tinted windows crept by the house heading west. Jessica walked to the front yard. The car turned the corner stopping behind the Lightning Electrical van. Alain emerged from it looking even more fit out of uniform if that was possible. His black t-shirt clung to his broad shoulders and muscular chest. And that didn't begin to describe how his tight, faded jeans covered his lower half. Jessica licked her lips. He looked delicious. His expression changed and she turned to see Steve round the corner of the house.

"Hi," she said. "This is Steve. He's giving me a quote on getting the house wired."

"I know who he is," Alain growled.

The look on his face changed again. Now it was murderous.

"I-I've got to run," Steve stammered. "I'll get the numbers crunched and have the quote to you in a day or two." He rushed away.

"Obviously some bad blood between you two." Jessica wiped her sweaty palms on her thighs.

"That's the understatement of the century. That bastard killed my wife." He clenched and unclenched his fists as he seethed.

Hadn't Mrs. Bell said Alain's wife killed herself? If that was correct, what did Steve have to do with it?

"But didn't your wife …"

"Commit suicide?" he interrupted before she could finish her sentence. "Yes, but if it hadn't been for him being drunk and hitting her that night, she wouldn't have. Melanie would still be alive."

Jessica hugged him hoping to take some of his hurt away.

His hard, hot – temperature and sexy – body felt good pressed against hers.

10

Alain wrapped his arms around her. He'd not held a woman in his arms since before Melanie's accident. After that, she didn't let him anywhere near her. His right hand traced down Jessica's back. He gripped her perky bottom in his hand and pulled her closer. He caressed her cheek with the backs of his fingers, tipped her head back with his thumb and forefinger, and kissed her.

A crow cawed from close by. Jessica stiffened and pulled away. Her eyes filled with fear and the flush from their closeness faded. It squawked again and Jessica darted into the house. She couldn't be afraid of birds, could she?

"Go on, get out of here," he yelled at the sleek, black, feathered creature sitting on the eaves.

The crow cocked its head from one side to the other all the while not taking its eyes off him. The damn thing was sizing him up. It stretched out its wings, flapped and folded them back into place with a shake. Its behaviour unnerved Alain. He, who was a cop and had to remain calm and in control.

As he walked to the front door, the bird hopped along the roof following him. Finally, it flew up to the top of the lightning rod on the peak of the turret roof. If only a storm would blow in and a bolt of electricity strike the crow and fry the thing to a crisp. Alain gave it the finger and cursed it for ruining what might have been with Jessica a few short moments ago.

"Jess, you okay?" he called walking through the front door.

She didn't answer. He locked up from the inside and searched for her beginning on the main floor. No sign of her here so he tried upstairs. He found her in the attic sitting cross-legged on the floor amongst paint flakes and chips, her back to the turret windows.

Alain sat down beside her. Without saying a word, he leaned over to kiss her. Before his mouth reached hers, the doorbell rang. That same irritating sound of a bicycle bell reverberated through the house.

11

Jessica checked her watch and scrambled to her feet. "That's the guy about removing the lead paint. I've got to meet him," she apologized then turned and bounded down the stairs.

Breathless when she got to the main floor, she took a moment to stop wheezing before she opened the front door. "You must be Brad?"

"Yup. That's me."

"I was up in the attic when you rang the bell," she commented brushing paint flakes off the seat of her jean shorts.

The short, stocky man in front of her had salt and pepper hair, and was clean-shaven. He didn't appear to be much taller than Jessica. He bent down and picked up one of the curls from the floor and rubbed it between his fingers then dropped it.

"Start in the kitchen?" She wasn't up to climbing all those stairs so soon after descending from the attic. At least a wander around on the main level first would give her knees a chance to recover.

"Sounds fine." He pulled a small notebook and stubby pencil out of his shirt pocket.

Before Jessica could show the man to the kitchen, Alain appeared at the top of the stairs. "I'll leave and let you get on with it," he said.

Brad looked up in the direction of the voice. "If this is lead paint, you two shouldn't be in here stirring it up."

"I know. Art and Bill have both told me the same thing. But there's work I need to get done and I've been meeting contractors here to get quotes. I've tried not to disturb things too much," Jessica replied.

Alain jogged down the steps and kissed her on the cheek. "I'll call you later."

"Please stay. I want you to. After everything being more of a problem and more expensive to fix than I envisioned, I need a shoulder to lean on." She turned her attention back to Brad Foster.

Unlike Steve from Lightning Electrical, this man didn't have a company logo on his clothes or wear a uniform of any kind. He wore a golf jersey and faded relaxed-fit jeans held up by a worn leather belt.

With Alain by her side, Jessica waited at the kitchen door. She watched the man work his way around the room, feeling the paint, and inspecting his hands afterwards. He scribbled something in his book before moving on to the dining room.

His routine didn't vary until he reached the fireplace room. The high wainscoting prevented him from feeling the walls. He cleared his throat umpteen times, making Jessica worry about what he was seeing and how much it would cost in the end.

"Definitely lead paint," he said when he finished his inspection of the house.

***

Alain put his arm around Jessica and pulled her close. "This isn't turning out the way you had planned, is it?"

"Far from it. I knew I would have to clean the place but every time I turn around, I find something else wrong that I have to deal with. I should just give up. Sell up and cut my losses like every owner before me has done."

"Hey, this defeatist isn't the Jessica, I've come to know and … admire." He almost said that four-letter word. He had never told any woman, other than Melanie, that he loved her. Did he love Jessica? He enjoyed spending time with her. She infuriated him with her stubborn, headstrong manner. He wanted to protect her. But love? It was way too soon for that, wasn't it? Most likely it was a case of lust. After all, he'd gone a long time without having sex.

He brought her hand to his mouth and kissed it. It was freezing. He surrounded hers with his large, warm ones.

"Please, don't start," she begged.

"I don't know what you're talking about."

"Outside, in the yard." She bowed her head.

"Oh that." He lifted her chin and looked into her eyes. "If you're not ready – if you think things are moving too fast."

"Not me. But you," she whispered.

He stood back. "You let me worry about me. I wouldn't have kissed you if I'd thought it was too soon after Melanie. I admit the time and place weren't the greatest. Seeing Steve brought it all back. I want to move on and I think I've found the person I want to do that with. I've thought of no one else these past few days."

***

Unable to process what Alain had just said to her, Jessica dashed to the turret room. She stared out the window while trying to come to grips with what he had said. It wasn't the *L* word but it was pretty close. Finding someone to move on with and she was the one. Her lips curled into a contented smile.

Creaking metal echoed through the empty room. Jessica stiffened. The door to the widow's walk steps opened. Footsteps on the hardwood floor got louder, as if someone approached. But she was alone. Alain was downstairs. Footprints appeared in the dust on the floor. Woman's footprints. She watched the marks as whoever created them walked to the stairs. The footfalls grew faint as the person descended.

"Alain," she cried. "I-I need you."

By the time he reached her side, tremors shook her body. She stood with her arm outstretched pointing at the shoe imprints. "L-look."

"What?"

"D-don't you see them?"

He hugged her to him. "What am I supposed to be seeing?"

Jessica burst into tears. He didn't see what she did and didn't believe her. That was far worse than not seeing.

A loud crash came from the window behind them. The

pane shattered. Blood smeared the surface. The crow with the single white feather hung limp, its beak trapped in the hole it created when it struck the glass.

Moments later, it thrashed against the windowpane. "Do something," Jessica screeched.

Alain picked up a block of wood and pressed it against the end of the bird's beak pushing it out of the broken window. It cawed and flew up to the roof.

"Why is that crow out to get me?" she lamented.

"What do you mean?" he led her away from the window and sat her down on the floor before sliding down the wall to sit beside her.

Jessica related her incident with the murder of crows – the one bird in particular. It acted like the leader. She did not believe in reincarnation but what if, what if it was Melanie? It fit. The bird appeared when she and Alain kissed outside. But it did not explain the previous encounter. The only thing the two events had in common was he had helped her the day she arrived. It could be the reawakening of his dead wife, determined to see he doesn't find someone else.

"After you ran off into the house, that damn bird watched me. Tracked me with its beady, black eyes."

Did she mention her theory to him? No, better keep it to herself for now. If she was to have any hope of a relationship with her hunky cop, it was best not to say a word. She'd wait it out and see if anything else happened. See if she had any more close encounters of the feathered kind.

She rested her head on his upper arm and flexed her fingers. They ached from balling them in a fist when the phantom footsteps walked through the room.

The window broken by the crow looked worse than the grimy panes of the others. With the blood being on the outside, she couldn't clean it. That window didn't open from inside unlike some of the others in the attic. Not that she should be in the house anyway. And now, it was another one she would have to replace.

Sniffling and snotting, she wiped her nose on her sleeve. Jessica sobbed and buried her face in Alain's chest. Today had been too much. She wanted out of here. Maybe she should be like everyone else who bought this place and put it back on the market. Chalk it up to experience and walk away.

"You're tired. Let me take you back to Cliffside."

"I can manage."

"No you can't. I am going to take you there. You're going to get yourself cleaned up and I am taking you out for a meal. No arguments."

She looked up at him and smiled. He had a way about him that made her want to take orders from him. "Okay, I agree to the meal but I'll take my car back to the Bell's. You go home and clean up, too, and then you can come and pick me up. Say an hour?"

"You drive a hard bargain, Jessica Maitland.

12

When Jessica entered her room at the guesthouse, the cardboard boxes containing her clothes were gone. She opened the closet doors. Her blouses, skirts and pants hung inside. She checked in the dresser drawers and her sweaters, and intimate apparel were all put away, too.

Pulling top after top out of the closet and flinging it on the bed, Jessica finally chose a long-sleeved, black satin blouse. It would need ironing before she could wear it. She found her favourite skinny jeans, and a pair of black, leather – vinyl – flats.

Alain was to pick her up in an hour. She still had to shower, apply makeup, do her hair, and now iron. There wouldn't be time for luxuriating in the soaker tub. She would have to settle for a quick shower.

The only things she hadn't seen in her room were an iron and ironing board. She couldn't ask Eunice to press her clothes for her but she would ask to use them herself.

After showering, applying makeup and drying her hair, Jessica wrapped the long terry cloth robe around her and put on her slipper booties. She took her clothes downstairs. "Can I use your iron and ironing board?" she asked.

"I thought I heard you come in. Going someplace nice?"

"I'm not sure where Alain is taking me," she replied. "I just know he's picking me up here in – egad – half an hour."

Mrs. Bell bustled about in the kitchen hauling out the items Jessica had requested. "You go finish getting ready. I'll do this for you."

"No. It's all right. I can do it," she replied setting her jeans on one end of the ironing board and preparing her shirt at the other. It took some time to do the blouse because of the fabric. While she finished pressing her jeans, the doorbell rang.

Jessica looked at the wall clock in the kitchen. He was early.

"Come in, Constable Fournier, although since you're not in uniform, I guess I can call you Alain," Eunice said. "Jessica is in the kitchen. Come on through."

Jessica flushed with embarrassment when Alain entered the room. They had only known each other a minute and here she was in just a housecoat in front of him. His appearance didn't help the awkwardness either. Dressed in a wine coloured dress shirt and slim fitting black pants, he looked gorgeous. Every bit as much as in his jeans and tight black t-shirt. With his sleeves rolled a couple of turns up his forearms, it looked classy yet casual.

"I-I'll get dressed and be right with you," she stammered.

"Take your time. I'm a bit early."

Discombobulated by seeing him, she shuffled out of the room. She wanted to flee as fast as possible but her body and mind were not communicating.

Jessica leaned against the closed bedroom door trying to catch her breath and get over her humiliation. When the feeling passed, she got dressed, grabbed her handbag off the bed and went back downstairs.

"Will I do?" she asked walking into the kitchen.

Alain whistled. "I'll say."

"Have a lovely evening, you two."

"Thanks, Mrs. B." Alain opened the front door for Jessica and stood aside as she walked out. "I won't keep her out too late," he quipped then turned and winked at her.

Jessica's cheeks warmed. He pushed her buttons like no one ever had before. When they reached the car, he opened the door, waited for her to get in and settled. She'd never had a man treat her so well. Even her ex-husband never held a door for her, not even when she was pregnant.

***

Alain eased in behind the wheel and fastened his seatbelt. It had been too long since he'd been out with a woman. Since Melanie's death, he worked or holed himself up in the house like a hermit. Sure, Jessica drove him mad at times, but he liked spending time with her. Whether it would be a serious relationship, or not only time would tell.

"Where are we going?" she asked.

"Huh? Oh sorry. There's a good place down the highway a couple of miles. The pizza is their signature dish. Do you like pizza?"

"Love it."

He breathed a sigh of relief. Not everyone liked Italian, let alone pizza. Backing the car out of the Bell's driveway, Alain drove east along Royal Avenue. Jessica's house looked ominous in the darkness. He shifted into a lower gear before driving down the thirteen percent grade, taking the corner with caution.

When he reached the highway, he stole a glance at his companion while waiting for the light to change. She looked beautiful in the gloaming. Her red hair shone and her blue-green eyes sparkled. She turned to him and smiled.

The red light Gods were with him tonight. Every traffic light turned red as he approached. It amazed him how much of a difference it made when that happened. Under normal circumstances, it took three or four minutes. Tonight it took over twice as long. Ten minutes later, he pulled into the parking lot at Luigi's.

"We're here," he announced pulling into a parking spot and turning off the engine.

***

Jessica peered through the windshield. The place was nothing to look at on the outside – dive was a more apt description of the place. Still, she trusted Alain's judgement. It couldn't be as bad inside, could it?

He helped her out of the car and put his arm around her shoulders. She felt safe next to him, not that she had any reason to feel frightened. The incident with the crows was freaky. The footsteps and footprints in the dust were, too. But tonight they weren't anywhere near Hillcrest House. They were in the next town.

Jessica stepped through the door. She was wrong. This place could be as bad on the inside. She shuddered. Colourful paper lanterns hung from every inch of the ceiling. Chianti bottles in baskets hung on the walls. The Jacquard paper looked greasy and grimy from years of cooking and frying.

A bleached blonde server in a too-short skirt led them to a booth in a secluded corner. Jessica smiled inside. This was the one good thing to come out of the night so far. A bottle of Valpolicella and two glasses appeared on their table. Alain poured each of them a glass, hers being more generous. But he was a police officer and driving, she reasoned.

She leaned against the seat back, spinning her glass back and forth by the stem between her fingers.

Alain leaned forward and put his hands over hers. “You know my baggage. I know you have some. Everyone comes with a certain amount. Why don’t you tell me?”

“You don’t want to hear it.”

“I know you’re hiding something.”

She sighed. He was a cop, after all. His instincts would tell him she had secrets. “I’m divorced and my ex is a bastard.”

“Okay, that’s a start. Your baggage can’t be worse than mine. A drunk driver hit my wife’s car and she killed herself not long afterwards. What isn’t now and has never been public knowledge is Melanie was pregnant when Steve smashed into her that night. She lost her leg and the baby – a boy – that night.”

“Oh, Alain I’m so sorry. I didn’t know.” Jessica swallowed. “I had a child – a little girl. She died of crib death. My husband, now ex, blamed me for her death. I suffered from post-partum depression. I didn’t know it at the time. Wasn’t diagnosed until it was too late. But I felt tired all the time, suicidal at times and couldn’t bond with my little girl.”

A tear escaped and ran down her cheek. Alain reached over and brushed it away with his thumb. He pried her left hand away from her wine glass and kissed it.

The delivery of their pizza prevented things from going any further. A server brought it to their table on its pan atop an elevated cake plate. Another restaurant employee followed and offered to grate fresh Parmesan over it.

Their conversation paused while they ate. Alain refilled Jessica's wine glass when she emptied it.

"Should I order another bottle?" he asked.

"No. You need your license for your job and I don't need to have a hangover tomorrow."

"Fair enough."

While they finished, a couple of men carrying beer bottles sauntered over to the table. "Hey Al, who's the chick?" the one standing by Jessica asked.

She felt the blush start at her toes and rush to the top of her head.

"Manners, boys, manners," Alain said standing.

Was he going to take them both on to defend her honour? A barroom brawl, while the location suited it, was the last thing she wanted.

"If you two morons can act like gentlemen for a minute, I'll introduce you." He turned to her. "I work with these two. Jess, this is Chuck, one-half of our canine unit. The dog is the better looking of the two," he chided. "And this is Jake, one of our forensics team. Guys, this is Jessica."

Before she could object, the two sat down at the free spots at their table. The banter between them and Alain continued although they did tone it down to a respectable level. The bartender looked their way a number of times. Jess caught him nodding towards a huge, burly black man – presumably the bouncer.

Alain's coworkers both sported beer bellies. It was obvious they drank on a regular basis and were well on the way to having a skin full now. Despite loving dogs, and one of the cops a dog handler she didn't look forward to striking up a conversation with either of them.

"I think you pair have had enough. Let me …"

Please no. Don't offer them a ride home. Two drunks in the car belching, farting, and maybe puking was disgusting. Alain kept his car immaculate. Cleaning up after them would be unfair to him.

"… Call you a cab," he finished.

Jessica breathed a sigh of relief. That was one bullet dodged.

***

Alain returned to the table ten minutes later. "Sorry about that. They aren't a bad pair. You happened to see them at their worst. Must have had a rough shift. That does it, as in drives us to drink, to us all at some point." He reached across the table and took her left hand in both of his. "Now where were we?"

"I want to leave. Go back to Cliffside. I'm tired and have a million things to deal with before morning."

This was not how he imagined his night out with Jessica ending. He envisioned them going back to his place, opening another bottle of wine and cuddling on the sofa. He had hoped it would end with them making love but that didn't look like a possibility now.

After paying the bill, he walked her in the direction of the car. Before they got there, he turned the corner around the building. The full moon was low in the sky. Its reflection in the water sparkled like diamonds.

"It's beautiful," she whispered. "Thank you for showing me."

Alain lifted her chin with his fingers and kissed her lips. He tasted the lingering flavours of their meal. When he brushed his tongue against her teeth, she opened her mouth to receive it.

He traced his fingers down her neck to the collar of her blouse. Even though she hadn't tucked it into her jeans, he unbuttoned it with his right hand. She shivered and her skin came up in goosebumps. Alain held her closer to him. A car pulled around the side of the building catching them in the beams of the headlights.

***

Embarrassed by the situation, Jessica scrambled behind him. She fumbled with her blouse to button it. After the car door closed, alarm beeped and headlights shut off, she emerged from her hiding place.

Alain burst into laughter.

"What's so funny?" she demanded.

"You," he howled.

Jessica looked down at herself. She pulled the bottom of her blouse away from her body so she could see. In her haste to fasten her shirt, she had done it wrong. She had missed a buttonhole. Now her blouse was longer on one side than on the other, and the shorter side puckered at the neck. "I'd like to go home, please." She stomped back to the car.

When Alain caught up with her, he turned her around and kissed her again. It was no good. The mood was gone. Between getting caught in the parking lot and him laughing at her, she wanted no part of making out.

Ten minutes later, they pulled into the driveway at Cliffside Guest House. Alain exited first and walked around the car to open her door. Tempted to fling it open and hit him where it counts, she thought better of it. The evening hadn't been that bad. And if it came right down to it was she ready for a relationship with him? She wanted more than a one-night stand but did he? Perhaps the car coming along and catching them in the headlights was a blessing. Standing on the shore of the river under the light of the moon was dead romantic though.

Alain walked her to the door and kissed her good night. "I'll call you tomorrow," he said before returning to his car.

Jessica stayed on the front step and watched until his vehicle disappeared from sight. Maybe she'd been too hasty getting into a mood when he laughed at her. Did she ruin things between them with her anger? She hoped not. Taking a deep breath, she took out her key and opened the front door.

"Good night with Constable Fournier?" Mrs. Bell asked when she entered the hall from the living room.

Jessica nodded then darted up the stairs to her room.

13

The following morning, Jessica sat at the dining room table at Cliffside Guest House. The disarray of paperwork spread out in front of her. It looked like the repairs could get started on her place by the end of the week. She'd ordered locksets and deadbolts and Wilf would install them when they came in. She picked up the quote from Art Smith again and sighed. She'd already given him the go ahead along with a deposit and he would be able to start in a few days. The roadblock now was waiting for the lead paint removal.

Jessica had hoped to receive the quote for the electrical work by now but still nothing. Should she even entertain having Lightning Electrical rewire the mansion? Given the bad blood between Alain and Steve, maybe she should hire another contractor. By the same token, this company was on the list of tradesmen recommended by Mr. Bell.

She tidied her stack of papers and took a sip of her coffee. When her cell phone rang, she dropped the cup onto the saucer. The hot drink spilled onto the pile of documents. Patting the forms with her napkin, she sopped up the mess. Only the brown stain remained.

The shrill ringtone continued. Pressing the talk button, Jessica snapped, "Hello."

"Brad Foster here. Did I catch you at a bad time?"

"Sorry. Didn't mean to bite your head off."

"I hope you're sitting down. I've been over the numbers and went back over them again."

Great. She knew where this conversation was going and didn't like it. "Give me the bad news."

"We're looking at upwards of twenty grand."

"T-twenty thousand dollars?" she stammered.

"Afraid so."

Jessica choked back a sob. She didn't have that kind of money. Even if she sold everything she owned, other than Hillcrest House, she still couldn't afford the job. "I'm going to have to get back to you. It's a lot of money. Can you email me the numbers? I'll need to have something on paper."

"Certainly. You take all the time you need to think this through."

Not that Brad could see but Jessica nodded. She gave him her email address and disconnected the call. Her dream home had become a money pit. No wonder she got it for such a low price. The bank loaned her the money for the mortgage. Would they also lend her an additional forty thousand? Surely, that would be enough to cover the electrical work on top of the other things. It might even leave her a bit of money for decorating. Dejected, she trudged up the stairs to her room and flopped onto the bed.

About an hour later, she woke to the red light on her cell phone blinking. The email from Brad containing his quote was in her inbox along with the one from Lightning Electrical. The latter one scared her. When he visited the house, Steve never gave any idea how much he thought the work would cost.

Jessica rolled off the bed and turned on her laptop. Wanting to get the bad news over with, she opened the email from the electrician first. Seventy-five hundred dollars for the upgraded service and new electrical panel plus fixtures, switches, receptacles and covers if she wanted anything other than the basic style. If the chandeliers, ceiling lights and the lamp mounted on the newel post could be re-used, she wouldn't have to pay extra to have them bought and installed.

It was still too early to phone the bank to try to arrange a loan for the extra money. Jessica composed an email and attached all the quotes to it. Not wanting to sound desperate, even though she was, she read and re-read the email and tweaked it each time. She finished by saying she would phone at eleven o'clock to discuss things and hit send. Now it was a waiting game.

***

Jessica entered the kitchen. The growling, gurgling sounds of the coffeemaker indicated a fresh pot. She poured herself a mug and leaned against the counter. The bank wouldn't refuse her request to borrow more money, would they? She hoped not. Her business, when she worked, did quite well. Being a freelance graphic designer meant she could work anywhere although having an office to work out of did help. Jessica did most of the work on the computer but she still liked to sketch out her ideas on paper first. Her drafting table was somewhere in the outbuildings at Cliffside. If she had it, she could get a lot of work done while the house project was on hold. Still, she would not ask the Bells if she could set it up in their house. They'd been good enough to her already.

Eunice appeared on the terrace and Jessica went outside to join her. The morning sun still low in the sky, warmed the patio, even under the porch roof. She sat in one of the chairs at the cast iron bistro table and watched Mrs. Bell fuss over her plants, picking dead leaves off here, a spent bloom there, as she watered them.

Not wanting to startle the woman, Jessica cleared her throat before speaking. "Your flowers are lovely."

"Thank you, dear."

"I'd love it if you would help me with the plantings at Hillcrest House. I can't do anything next to the walls because there's too much repair work needs doing to the lattice under the verandah." She stood and walked to the urn the woman hunched over.

"I'd be happy to do that," Mrs. Bell replied as she continued working.

"Do you know anything about the fountain in the front yard there?"

"Other than it's there and I don't ever recall seeing it running." Eunice straightened up. "That's better. My poor old back can't take all the bending." She walked to the table and sat down.

Jessica joined her. Getting the water feature running again

would add to the curb appeal of the house. With any luck, the water supply to it was shut off and it wasn't anything more costly. She would have to check with her insurance company. Maybe that was why the previous owners never had it operational. Swimming pools raised the premiums so it made sense it would, too.

Her cell phone chirped. She had set the alarm to go off shortly before she was to call the bank. "Wish me luck. I've sent off all the quotes for the work that I need to get done at Hillcrest House. I'm to call the loans officer at eleven. It's almost that now."

***

Inside the house, Jessica headed straight to her room. She had all the quotes printed except for the one from Lightning Electrical. She wanted to have it at her fingertips along with the others. She'd left her email running earlier so found the one from the electrician and opened it. The bank would want to discuss the costs with her before saying yay or nay.

Two minutes to go, at least according to the clock on her computer. Scrolling through the contacts on her phone, she found the desired one and pressed the button. While she waited for the call to go through, Jessica got comfortable at the dressing table. She then arranged the printouts so that she could see the name of the sender at a glance.

"Cascades National. Donna speaking, how can I direct your call?"

"Hi Donna, it's Jessica Maitland. I sent you some quotes this morning and said I'd call you at eleven. I just wondered if you had a chance to look them over yet."

"Yes. I got them. You're looking to get an additional forty thousand dollars on top of your mortgage you have with us."

"Exactly." Jessica stiffened. Donna sounded far more business-like than in her previous dealings.

"What do you propose to use for collateral?"

"A fully restored Victorian mansion," she replied.

"A Victorian mansion which you've mortgaged to the tip

of the lightning rod on its turret."

Jessica didn't want to beg for the funds but with the direction the conversation headed in, she thought she might have to do just that. She propped her elbow on the dressing table, leaned her forehead into her hand, and massaged her temple with her fingertips. "I know it is but the sooner I get the extra funds, the sooner I can get the work completed and I can move in and re-establish my business."

"That's another thing. You're currently not working. I realize you're self-employed but …."

"I can't get back to work properly without a functional office. I can do some of the things like stock image, book cover designs but that's it. I have some requests from prospective customers," she answered, her voice louder than she intended. "You have to understand my frustration. I had no idea the house was in this state of disrepair when I bought it. Everything pointed to a clean, empty, move-in ready house."

"Given the situation, I'm going to have to discuss this additional loan with my superiors. I'll let you know by the end of the day."

"Thanks," Jessica mumbled. "I'll even invite you to my housewarming and you'll be able to see the money wasn't wasted. Hillcrest House will be beautiful again. I guarantee it," she babbled.

The loans officer had hung up. Disappointed, Jessica disconnected the call. End of business today. That's what Donna told her. She picked up her neatly arranged quotes and tossed them into the air.

Picking up her jacket, Jessica jammed her arms into the sleeves and grabbed her keys off the dressing table. She snatched her camera and handbag and stormed out of the house. The mood she was in, she did not want to be near anyone she cared about lest she blow up and offend. Furious, she wanted to get away from Hillcrest House and Angel Falls.

***

When she accelerated, Jessica squealed the tires leaving

trails of rubber on the road behind her. She drove for miles before calming down. Once she did, she began looking for a place to turn around. The road turned towards the river. A bridge spanned the water leading to the far shore. Following the signs, she found herself out on an island.

The tranquil and unspoilt landscape improved her mood. Before long, she found herself enjoying the day. Signs for a chocolate shop piqued her curiosity. When she approached the entrance to the parking lot, she turned on her signal light and pulled in.

People sat at patio tables on the terrace enjoying the warm weather drinking coffee or eating ice cream. Jessica wondered if it was homemade on site. Stepping through the door, she inhaled the aroma of chocolate that filled the air. A sample bar stood off to the left with disposable, plastic tongs to use. After tasting some of the products, she meandered through the store into the ice cream parlour section. She bought a dark chocolate cone and took it outside to a grassy area with picnic tables to enjoy the sweet treat.

The entire village was quaint. It was as if time stood still. Hillcrest House would be quite at home in this setting. Where it currently stood, newer homes and some brand new construction surrounded it. At one time, the property had to be much larger and over the years, severed and smaller lots sold off.

Refreshed and contented, Jessica pulled out her camera and went for a walk. She stopped at a signpost in the parking lot and noticed that she could drive all the way around the island. But first, an exploration of the village to take photographs was in order. Tall trees and centuries old homes lined the streets.

She turned left onto Church Street. Many of the houses were newer than on the main road through the village. A golf course ran along the right side of the street. The walk was longer than expected, but the appearance of the steeple on the old stone church rewarded Jessica. A cemetery was on a narrow road, which she thought was only a parking lot for the church. Through the trees, she saw that the golf course she'd glimpsed earlier encroached on the graveyard.

After returning to her car, Jessica enjoyed driving around the island stopping at local craft and antique shops. With her finances being in the state they were in, buying was not an option.

By the time she returned to Cliffside Guest House, it was almost six o'clock. Pulling her phone out of her purse, she discovered she had one missed call. It was Donna from the bank. Damn! Jessica fired up her laptop and opened her email. While it chugged along, she drummed her fingers on the dressing table. The usual assortment of adverts, offers and other junk cluttered her inbox. The last message to download was the one she wanted. The one that would make or break her. Squinting and looking away from the screen as if afraid something would jump out and attack her, she clicked on the message. She had to read it a few times before the words sunk in. "Woo hoo," she hollered into the empty room. "Yes!" She pumped her fist in the air. Donna had come up trumps for her – again.

Get the Lead Out. Jessica had to call Brad Foster and get him on site as soon as possible. She dropped to her knees and fumbled through the papers she'd thrown on the floor earlier. Funny, Mrs. Bell hadn't seen to her room today. If she had, her bed would be made and the emails picked up and put on the dressing table. She hoped Eunice was all right.

First things first. She found the quote she was looking for and placed the call. Brad could start on Monday. Breathing a sigh of relief, Jessica headed downstairs to seek out Eunice. She found the woman bustling about the kitchen. After the mood she left the house in that morning, Mrs. Bell likely thought better of invading her space.

The weekend crawled by. Alain worked twelve-hour overnight shifts. He called her every day before he went on duty promising he would make things up to her on his next day off. She looked forward to spending time with him. Now that her loan had gone through, she'd be over at Hillcrest House supervising the workers.

14

On his way to Hillcrest House, Brad stopped by Cliffside and picked up a key from Jessica. He didn't want her near the place when he was working. Yes, he took precautions but didn't want to take any unnecessary chances.

After he backed his van in to the driveway, he climbed out and opened the rear doors. He had stowed everything he needed the night before. He would have liked to get closer to the front door but did not want to drive on the lawn.

Loaded down with a toolbox in each hand, Brad walked to the front door and left them on the verandah. He retraced his steps many times before he had everything he needed for the job assembled there.

He planned to start in the attic and work his way down, giving each room a thorough clean when he'd finished. Then he'd do a complete top to bottom scrubbing at the end of the job of the entire house. At least the room on the top level of the mansion had no furniture in it making it the easiest one to do. The possessions in the others would slow the work down. Not only would he have to seal the rooms but everything inside them, too. The sheets covering the trappings would require disposal and everything vacuumed and washed down. He hated charging the amount he quoted but with all the extras involved, it was fair.

Before entering the house, Brad donned a paper boiler suit and pair of shoe covers. His heavy rubber gloves and respirator were in the same toolbox from where he'd pulled the protective clothing. When he opened the door, a cold, clammy draft greeted him. He passed it off as the lack of central heating and the rain over the weekend. Once he got working, he'd never notice it. He moved all his equipment into the foyer then locked up.

He hefted the roll of plastic onto his right shoulder, grabbed his bucket, picked up his toolbox with his other hand and climbed up the stairs to the attic. Winded when he reached the top floor, he waited until he caught his breath before trudging back down to the main level for his other toolbox that contained rolls of duct tape, sponges and scrapers, and his industrial shop vac with a HEPA filter.

He could draw water from the bathroom on the second floor. Before he went any further, he went downstairs and filled his bucket. At least when he got the attic finished, he wouldn't have to do steps to get water; same when he did the first floor. He had the kitchen on that level.

A generator in the back of the van provided electricity. Brad ran a one hundred foot extension cord out one of the windows and connected it at each end. It was just long enough. He might have to daisy chain a couple together to achieve the length he would need for other parts of the house. He started by vacuuming the loose paint flakes that littered the floor. Once he'd completed that task, he sealed off the room. Brad spent the rest of the day removing the flaking paint from the walls and ceiling, and cleaning up afterwards. He rolled up the plastic keeping the debris contained, placed it into a large garbage bag then tied it shut.

At the end of the day, Brad moved his equipment down one floor, collected the trash bag from the attic and grabbed an extra one. In the foyer, he took off the boiler suit and shoe covers and put them in the second sack he brought downstairs.

***

When he returned the following morning, Brad brought in half a dozen boiler suits sealed in individual packages along with a box of paper booties. He decided to start in the room over the kitchen despite it being chock-a-block with furniture. This would be the case with the rest of the house. There was no draft when he laid out the plastic sheeting to cut it. Before he could retrieve his utility knife, the loose end billowed up from the floor and over the roll. After the third time it happened, he heard children's laughter.

Everyone in Angel Falls knew of Hillcrest House's reputation, including Brad. "Okay, quit playing silly beggars and let me get on with my work," he scolded. The giggling stopped and the sheet remained unmoved on the floor.

Without any more phantom breezes, it still took the better part of two hours to move the furniture to the center of the room, get it covered in plastic and sealed.

Brad had estimated one day per room but this one and maybe some of the others would take over two days to complete.

When he quit for the day, he had only completed half of the large room. He did not want to clean up and have to start from scratch. He grabbed the roll of plastic and the duct tape and sealed the room from the outside. The only thing to do the next morning would be to tape up the doorway once he was inside. He could live with that.

***

When Brad stepped into the hallway the next morning, the garbage bag he had sealed shut from doing the attic lay split open. Its contents scattered across the floor. His respirator, which he had placed with the rubber gloves, paper booties, and extra boiler suits, was missing. He scratched his head, positive he had locked up the previous night when he left. He figured an animal ripped the trash bag but that did not explain the whereabouts of his protective mask. He gathered up the mess and put it in a new large bin liner, sealed it and took it out to his vehicle. When he opened the back doors, the respirator he'd been using for the job hung by its strap from a hook on the side wall. Shaking his head, he plucked it from its hanging place, closed the vehicle up and locked it.

Despite it taking longer than the two weeks he'd estimated to complete the job, the rest continued without any further incidents to Brad's relief. Once he'd locked his equipment and waste materials in the van, he made sure the house was secure and returned the key to Jessica.

15

Now with the lead paint removed, the rest of the work on Hillcrest House could begin. Jessica phoned Steve, Art and Wilf to let them know. Art could come right away. Wilf, too. Steve was finishing a job but would be there by the end of the week.

Before leaving Cliffside that morning, Jessica gathered a broom, mop, plastic pails, sponges, cleaning supplies, and a couple of battery-operated camping lanterns from the things she'd stored at the Bell's. She stopped off and picked up a couple of bottles of Murphy's Oil Soap and a package of large green garbage bags. The woodwork and floors would shine once again after a good scrubbing with this.

When she reached the front door, Brad's *Lead Paint Removal – Do Not Enter* sign still hung in one of the panes of glass. She yanked it down and walked in. The house no longer smelled damp and stale. A citrus scent filled the air. Seeing the furniture no longer covered with sheets and looking clean surprised her.

She trudged up the stairs to the second floor leaving the buckets and cleaning products there before continuing to the attic level with the rest. Without electricity to heat the water, she would have to settle for cold and hoped the supply to the house wasn't shut off.

Jessica skipped back down the stairs empty-handed to get water from the bathroom. Placing one of the pails in the tub under the faucet, she turned it on. Nothing happened. She was about to turn it off when a huge spurt of air exploded from the spout followed by a trickle of water. The pipes in the wall rattled as another burst escaped. When it began to run, it was rusty brown. Jessica yanked the bucket out from under this dirty liquid and left it running until it ran clear.

With both buckets filled – one with a strong solution of Mr. Clean, she lumbered back upstairs. Starting at the far side of the attic, she mopped the floor surprised that it wasn't dirtier. Brad had to have cleaned the place after he removed the lead paint.

When she returned to the bathroom, children's laughter broke the silence. Jessica dropped the pails and ran in the direction of the sound. It came from the room over the kitchen but no one was there. It had to be her imagination. She was the only one in the house. The haunted house rumours were just that – rumours. There were no such things as ghosts. Besides, didn't all Victorian mansions have that same reputation? Haunted, schmaunted. Hillcrest House was no more haunted than the Bell's guesthouse.

Jessica returned to the bathroom. Steam covered the small mirror over the sink. Impossible when only the cold water worked. Writing appeared in the fog. *Death to all who live here.* A strangled scream escaped from her mouth. She stumbled backwards until she reached the bathtub and could go no further. Except she did. She lost her balance and fell into it. The harder she tried to extricate herself, the deeper she went. Like trying to get out of bed in the middle of the night with a Charley Horse in her leg and only succeeding in tangling herself up in the covers. Giving up, she pulled her feet in then stood up.

The next room she tackled was the one over the kitchen. The sheets that covered the furniture were gone. This was a child's bedroom at one time. Maybe even a nursery. When she turned around and saw a crib, she choked back a sob. Her knees weakened. She grabbed for the rocking chair to steady herself. It tipped over and Jessica landed hard on the floor.

Curling up in the fetal position, she cried. She sobbed until she had no tears left. She hadn't cried this much even when her own baby died. What was wrong with her? Drawing in a ragged breath, she got to her knees.

The room became clammy and cold. Children's laughter rang out. A small boy and girl stood in the far corner, pointing and giggling at her. One of them looked like the apparition that had appeared in her photograph of this room. She tried to scream but no sound came out. When she shrank back against the wall, the ghostlike presences vanished. The room returned to its previous temperature.

Who were these children? Did they live in the house at one time? Was this their nursery? Curiosity piqued, Jessica searched the room for clues. In the top drawer of the dresser, she found a package wrapped in blue tissue paper. With care, she lifted it out from its resting place and laid it on the bed.

She peeled the bundle open, revealing a white satin and lace, christening gown. Jessica couldn't believe it remained snow white, as if put away the previous day. She ran her hand over the delicate fabric. Her finger caught in something shiny at the neck of the dress. She tugged on it and out popped a long gold chain with a key affixed to it. It was too small to be a household lock. Maybe it belonged to a jewellery or a strong box.

Before continuing her search, she put the chain around her neck so she didn't lose it. Jessica found nothing else here and failed in the other areas she hunted through on this level. She left a path of destruction in her wake. The last room on the second floor was the one under the turret that opened out onto the balcony.

Jessica forged ahead. Nothing under the bed or in any of the drawers. She opened the wardrobe. Nothing there either. Feeling along the top shelf, her fingertips brushed against an object in the back corner. Too far back to grip. She dragged the stool away from the dressing table and climbed onto it. This had to be it.

Bringing it to the front of the shelf, Jessica climbed down. She lifted the small chest and blew off the dust. The box measured about ten inches wide, eighteen inches long and about ten inches deep with an elaborate fleur-de-lys carved in the lid. A brass hasp and lock secured the contents. She carried it over to the huge four-poster bed and dropped it onto the mattress, the weight being too much to carry any longer.

With shaking fingers, she took the chain from around her

neck, inserted the key into the lock, and turned it.

16

The lock opened. Excited to discover the contents of the wooden box, Jessica slid the padlock out of the hasp and lifted the lid. A yellowed newspaper lay on top. She took it out and unfolded it.

Angel Falls Freeholder May 2, 1910

OWNER DIES IN SAW MILL ACCIDENT – ESCAPES GRUESOME DEATH

Asher Hargrave died yesterday at the Angel Falls Saw Mill. Witnesses say he was on the upper level when the boards collapsed beneath him sending him crashing to the floor below. The fall broke his neck and he died instantly. The death could have been far more gruesome. Had he landed two feet further left, he would have fallen into the spinning saw blade.

Jessica cringed at the thought. Reading that made her break out in a sweat thinking how close the man came to falling into the machinery. Accompanying the piece was a photo of the deceased. She'd never been a good judge of age but thought he looked to be in his mid to late forties.

Angel Falls Freeholder June 30, 1910

WIDOW TAKES OWN LIFE AFTER LOSS OF HUSBAND

Local resident, Maggie Hargrave, despondent over the accidental death of her husband, Asher, at the local sawmill committed suicide by throwing herself off the roof of Hillcrest House.

It seemed the family lived in a shadow of death. The eldest children, twins Charles and Elizabeth, drowned in the river near the mouth of the stream below Angel Falls in July 1905. Their other daughter, Maggie, died of scarlet fever at the age of nine in 1903. A son, John, died in infancy of crib death in 1896.

Mrs. Hargrave spent time in the regional lunatic asylum after the drowning deaths of her children. Released after a two-year stay, the authorities believed she regained her previous good health.

It seems the death of her husband after losing her entire family was more than she could bear. Witnesses reported hearing an unearthly scream late at night from the area of Hillcrest House. When they went to investigate, the body of Maggie Hargrave lay pale and lifeless on the ground, her neck broken.

Who owned this box and the newspaper clippings contained therein? Maggie could have preserved the first one reporting Asher Hargrave's death. What about the other one? She couldn't clip her own death report from the newspaper. Who did? Another chill ran down her back and Jessica decided to put the papers away until another day.

When she returned them to the wooden box, a squawking crow swooped down and landed on the balcony railing. The cracked and bloodied beak identified it as the same bird that flew into the turret window the day Alain had taken her out for a meal. It held something in its mouth. Jessica opened the door and it flew off dropping the object on the floor. She bent down and picked up a wadded up piece of tinfoil from a cigarette package. Why did it bring her a present? Maybe her original theory of the crow being a reincarnation of Alain's dead wife was out to lunch? Or was it bang on and the crow was doing its best to drive her crazy? Was it thanking her and Alain for rescuing it from the window? At least this time it didn't fly at her in what she assumed was a rage.

Puzzling over the motive behind the gift, Jessica continued cleaning the second floor of the house. The heavy, antique, wooden furniture was far superior to what she had in storage at Cliffside. Maybe she would sell her things and keep this? Well, all but the mattress and box spring in the room where she found the box of newspaper clippings. She needed an office. A small room on the far side of the house on this level would work but she loved the room in the turret. She had set her heart on that part of the house from the time she first entered the attic level.

She returned to the bedroom where she found the box containing the newspaper clippings. She couldn't leave them behind and risk having them thrown out by a careless or uncaring worker.

***

When Alain arrived late in the afternoon, he found Jessica on the front steps holding a wooden box on her lap, her eyes red and puffy from crying. "What's wrong?" he asked, easing down beside her.

"I-I found this," she stammered. "It's so sad. It's filled with newspaper clippings about the Hargrave family. He died in an accident at his sawmill. Their children all died young."

He put his arm around her and pulled her close. It wasn't the first time they'd sat here doing just that and it likely wouldn't be the last.

17

When Jessica arrived the next day, ladders leaned against the house. Two pairs of sawhorses were set up in the side yard, one with a garbage can under it. "Good morning, Mr. Smith," she called, walking across the lawn.

"Ah, good morning to you, too." He whacked a windowpane with a rubber mallet sending broken glass into the waste bin below it.

"I'm really sorry but there's another window that needs repairing now. It's up in the turret. A crow flew into it a couple of weeks ago and smashed it."

"You mean this crow?" He pointed to the railing on the front verandah. "Crazy thing's been watching me all morning."

The bird cocked its head as if it understood the glazier's words. It flew from its perch over to the unoccupied set of sawhorses and cawed.

Looking around Jessica expected the murder of crows who had arrived the first time to fly in. The sky remained blue and bird free. Not a one on the wires or roof either. She breathed a sigh of relief.

The crow hopped over to the trestle holding the window frame and sidled its way to Jessica, touching her fingers with its beak. Startled, she yanked her hand away. The bird was not dissuaded. It touched her again. This time she remained still. The bird stretched its wings, folded them up and shook. The movements were hilarious.

"I think that bird likes you," Art commented. "Never seen the like in all my born days."

"It brought me something yesterday," Jessica answered. "It was only a piece of wadded up foil from a cigarette package but the crow dropped it on the balcony in front of me and watched me retrieve it."

"Well, I'll be," he whistled.

"What?"

Art nodded at the crow. It had worked its way over to Jessica and under her hand.

She cast her eyes downward, surprised to see she was stroking the bird's head. The feathers were soft. It wasn't gross like her mother told her growing up. *Don't touch that thing. It's filthy and infested with lice.* The woman's words echoed in her head. "I think you need a name," she said. "You're so sleek and black, well except for this crazy white feather stuck to your neck. No, that's a corny idea. I wish I knew if you were a male or female. It would make things easier for me." By now, she caressed it all the way down its back. "I think I'll call you Carol. Carol Crow. And if you turn out to be a male, you can be Carl."

The bird squawked leaving Jessica thinking it approved of its new identity before flying off. It returned about ten minutes later and dropped a bottle cap at her feet. This was the second gift it had given her. Okay, it wasn't much – tinfoil and now a bottle cap – but they were definitely presents.

18

The work on the mansion was now complete. It had taken longer than expected but in the end, worth the wait. Jessica wished she hadn't hired Steve to do the electrical work. With the hard feelings between him and Alain, it made a bad situation worse. The switch plate and light switch covers she'd chosen suited the age of the house even though the white, tamper resistant receptacles and rocker switches were modern. They complemented each other and didn't take away from the period style of the house.

With the wiring job finished, Jessica could cover the white primer with the colour coats. She decided on darker Victorian shades in keeping with the age of her home. At least the rich woodgrain remained stained and varnished. The Murphy's Oil Soap made it gleam again. But for now, the walls – at least on the second and attic levels – would remain as they were. Buying paint for the entire place wasn't an option. At least not until she got her business re-established in Angel Falls.

Jessica would only worry about the rooms on the main level. The wainscoting covered the lower two-thirds of the walls in all but the one sitting room. She wouldn't need to buy as much paint. Finding colours that wouldn't make the wood trim look orange was a challenge. The shutters on the windows didn't match the rest of the wood in the rooms. Jessica took them off and painted them the same off-white as the ceilings. The chandeliers sparkled when she turned them on. In the end, she chose a navy blue for the fireplace room, cranberry red for the hall, a creamy white for the dining room and colonial yellow for the other sitting room. Jessica painted the kitchen cabinets a high-gloss white and the walls sunbeam yellow. The room wasn't as bright and airy as the one at Cliffside Guest

House, but it was a marked improvement over what had been there before.

Jessica couldn't wait until the cooler weather so she could have a fire in the huge fireplace. Below the mantle, the two demonic brass heads with rings through their mouths leered at her. One must control the damper in the flue but which one? Other than to make it look symmetrical, what function did the second one serve? Did you turn, pull, pull and turn? She took hold of one of the rings and tried to turn it. It didn't budge. She pulled on it and the ring and part of the creepy face's mouth creaked and slid forward. A grinding noise filled the room.

19

A section of the outer wall where the wainscoting went all the way to the ceiling moved. It retracted and slid behind the wall towards the front of the house.

Stunned and excited, it took Jessica a moment to move. Regaining her senses, she scampered across the room and looked inside the concealed passage. A narrow set of stairs filled the room. A window near the top of the flight allowed light to filter in.

She stepped onto the first tread and pushed her foot down on it testing its strength. It seemed secure enough so she ascended pausing on each step. A small door stood at the head of the stairs. Turning the knob, she pushed on it. It didn't budge. She pulled on it. Still nothing.

Determined to find the location of the door, Jessica dashed down the stairs. She'd start in the space above the fireplace room. And if she could open it from the main level, it had to open from up there, too.

Funny, she'd not seen anything in there before. But then, she hadn't been looking either. Now, she had a rough idea where it should be – if it did open into that room. Maybe there was another passage there leading to the attic.

Excited about her discovery, Jessica charged upstairs and into the area over the fireplace room. There was no sign of a door. She looked out the bay window towards the one that looked into the hidden stairway then up the wall. The stone wall stood at least four feet further out than the wall inside the room. Why hadn't she noticed this anomaly before?

Running her hands along the wall and pushing against it at regular intervals, nothing gave in to the pressure. That meant the only place the door could be was behind the huge wardrobe. Jessica tried to move it but it was too heavy. She needed help. Where was Alain when she needed him?

***

"Jess, where are you?" Alain yelled from inside the front door. He glanced around the hall. Without the cobwebs, inch or so of dust and dirt, it almost looked like home. Jessica had done a lot in a short time, including getting under his skin. When his mind wasn't occupied with work, she was all he thought about. Hell, she even crept into his thoughts on the job.

"Up here."

He took the stairs two at a time. Once on the second floor, Alain poked his head in each room looking for her. When he found her, she was staring out the bay window.

"Look what I've found," she exclaimed. "It's a secret passage. Leads to this room – I think – but I can't figure out exactly where."

Alain joined her at the window.

"See? That window down there. It's not on the same level as the rest of the ones in the house. Come and I'll show you," she demanded grabbing his hand and leading him out of the room and downstairs.

Her hand was warm in his. His large hand dwarfed her small and delicate one.

When she opened the door to the fireplace room, a section of the opposite wall was missing.

"Well, I'll be damned," he mused scratching his head. Alain strode across the room and poked his head into the opening.

A thick layer of dust covered the stair treads except for where Jessica's footprints disturbed it. Cobwebs stretched across from one wall to the other and dust motes floated in the air trapped by the light coming in the small window.

Alain climbed the stairs leaving his large boot prints in his wake. Stopping at the porthole-like opening, he peered through the dust and grime before continuing to the door at the top.

"I couldn't get that door to open," Jessica called from the foot of the stairs.

Being bigger and stronger than she, he pushed hard against the door with his shoulder while turning the knob. It moved but not much. Something prevented it from opening further.

He trudged back down wiping the dust off his uniform shirt as he did. He passed Jessica at the bottom and returned to the room above by way of the main staircase. The only place the upper door could be, if it was in here, was behind the massive wardrobe.

"It moved a bit but not a lot," he said, standing at the top of the steps.

Alain marched back to the room where Jessica had shown him the window. Facing the wall where the hidden door should be, he pondered how best to move the huge cabinet. He decided the best course of action would be to sit down and try to push it with his legs and feet.

"Stand behind me and keep me from sliding when I try to move the wardrobe."

She complied. Alain got himself into position with his legs bent. Jessica pushed against his back, and he tried to straighten his legs. At first the heavy piece of furniture didn't move. Adhered to the floor like glue. He refused to give up and moved closer and tried again. This time, it slid about two feet but still not enough to reveal the passage entrance. They repeated the process until the wardrobe was in the corner of the room – well away from any hidden door – but there was no visible sign of it.

"Wait here. I'll go try it again from the other side. When it moves, slide something in to keep it from closing tight. Then we can open it the rest of the way from here."

"What should I use?" she asked folding her arms across her stomach.

"Try this." He took his truncheon out of his belt and handed it to her before disappearing out the door.

***

Jessica heard his footsteps in the hidden stairway. She held her breath in anticipation of the door opening.

"Stand back, Jess, just in case it flies open. Don't want you to get hurt," he yelled from his concealed location.

She backed up until she was about three feet away from the wall. The door could not be that wide. It hadn't seemed so when she first discovered it.

The wall moved about an inch. "I can see it," she exclaimed. "It's moving."

The next thing she knew, the door shot open with Alain stumbling behind.

"Wow," she whispered. It was the only word she could manage. With it wide open, Jessica saw the outline but there was no frame around it, no knob, and no sign of hinges from the bedroom. She peered around the opening and saw everything hidden on the secret side of the entrance.

But they used this staircase for what purpose? The servants couldn't have used it. They wouldn't have access to it, with it being off one of the main front rooms of the house. The maids, butler or footmen would have performed their duties as required and returned to the back of the dwelling and the kitchen. Even their sleeping quarters would have been in the attic. Maybe they did use this passage to get to the second floor out of sight then carried on to the third by way of those steps. That still didn't seem plausible. It made more sense for there to be another set of stairs off the kitchen and maybe all the way to the attic.

Jessica threw her arms around Alain's neck and hugged him. "Thank you, thank you, thank you," she cried.

20

After months of hard work, Hillcrest House was a showcase. Jessica strived for this since first buying the place. Tonight was her wine and cheese party. She'd invited her neighbours who had watched the progress from behind twitching curtains. She asked the tradespeople who worked on the house and their partners, the Bells and Alain, too.

Jessica scrubbed and polished every piece of wood in the mansion. She scrubbed and polished it again until it gleamed. The light from the chandeliers caught the facets on the crystals making it sparkle. She'd vacuumed and shampooed the upholstered furniture and area rugs. Everything had to be perfect.

Ensuring everything was spotless; Jessica paused at the foot of the main staircase. The figure of a woman in Victorian clothing floated up the stairs past her. When it reached the top, it turned and nodded. Was it the ghost of the unhappy Maggie Hargrave? If so, maybe she was finally at peace knowing someone occupied her former home and loved it as much as she did when she and Asher lived there.

The grandfather clock in the foyer chimed seven times. The guests would be arriving soon. Alain arrived first wearing the wine coloured shirt and black trousers he'd worn when they went to Luigi's.

A tray of flutes sat on the dining room table next to a bottle of champagne chilling in a clear ice bucket. Jessica designated Alain as her wine steward, at least for the first round. She removed platters of cheese from the fridge and arranged them on the table with the wines.

Boxes of assorted crackers lined her kitchen counter. Her invitation stated eight o'clock but there were always people who arrived early. Her original plan was to leave the biscuits in their packaging to keep them fresh but arranged them on plates and put them out with the other nibbles.

Standing in front of the dining room table, Jessica inventoried what she'd laid out. The only thing missing was the spreaders for the soft cheeses. When she tried to open the top middle drawer in the sideboard, it stuck. She tugged on it again and it finally opened bringing a yellowed piece of newspaper with it.

Angel Falls Freeholder June 6, 1908

LOCAL WOMAN MISSING – SEARCH CONTINUES

Lucille Walker, aged twenty-seven, was reported missing when she did not return to her place of employment after having been on leave for the previous week. Miss Walker was a domestic for Mr. and Mrs. Asher Hargrave.

The young woman was last seen boarding a westbound train at the Angel Falls station on May 25.

Witnesses say the young woman had the appearance of being heavily pregnant resulting in great consternation among the local population. Police are making inquiries and have circulated a photograph to other constabularies in the hope of finding her. A search of the local area achieved no results.

A photo accompanied the piece. Despite the poor quality, Jessica recognized the woman as the ghost who had passed her on the stairs earlier. It wasn't Maggie Hargrave after all. Jessica folded the clipping up and tucked it back in the drawer. She took out her set of knives with handles that looked like cheeses or crusty bread and placed them on the table near the platters. The glasses for the red and white wines were at either end of the table near the related bottles.

The doorbell rang. Jessica froze. "How do I look?" she asked, smoothing her royal blue cocktail dress.

"You look fine." Alain wrapped his arms around her waist. "Off you go. Your public awaits."

Jessica hurried to the front door. She paused at the mirror to check her makeup and ensure she didn't have lipstick on her teeth.

"Welcome, please come in." She ushered the first of her guests into the hall. "If you'd like to come through to the fireplace room," she instructed.

When everyone arrived and congregated in the room, Jessica excused herself and returned to the dining room and Alain. "You can pop the cork any time now. There's another bottle in the fridge if we need it."

"What did your last slave die of?" he chided before planting a kiss on her cheek.

Jessica jumped when he opened the champagne bottle. It sounded like a gunshot – not that she'd heard a lot of them.

Flutes filled, Jessica took the tray to the fireplace room and served everyone a glass. Standing with her back to the mantle, Jessica took hers in one hand and placed the salver on the coffee table with the other. "I'd like to thank you all for coming. A lot of hard work and tears have gone into making Hillcrest House a cozy home again. The contractors I hired have done a wonderful job. Thanks, Bill, for recommending them."

By now, Alain stood at her side. She turned to him. "Thank you, Alain. You've been my rock through all this. Every time I was ready to give up you were there for me. You dried my tears and gave me the occasional kick in the backside to get me moving forward again." Jessica smiled and mouthed 'I love you'. "So without further ado – I know you're anxious to see the rest of the house. To Hillcrest House," she toasted.

As Jessica circulated through the room chatting with her guests, a blood-curdling scream pierced the relative silence. Eunice pointed to the fireplace. Her champagne flute slipped from her fingers and shattered on the hardwood floor. The contents spilled onto the rug and shards of glass skittered everywhere. Her complexion lost all colour and she collapsed in a heap.

Jessica whipped around. Gliding about a foot above the floor was the figure of a man dressed in period costume. As she watched, he vanished through the wall at the entrance to the secret passage. Was he the ghost of Asher Hargrave? Did Eunice see him? After all, the woman said she didn't go in for all the rumours about Hillcrest House. Was that the reason she fainted?

21

Jessica knelt beside Mrs. Bell and held her hand. The woman's colour was no longer ashen. "I'm so sorry, my dear. I don't know what came over me. I've ruined your rug. Broken one of your lovely glasses."

"Don't worry about those things. I'm more concerned about you," she soothed stroking the back of the woman's hand.

"Get up, Eunice," Bill snapped. Unable to get down onto the floor beside his wife, he bent over her. "You're making a show of yourself."

"Mr. Bell," Jessica scolded.

Alain crouched on the other side of the stricken woman. "Jess is right, Mrs. B. Your health is far more important than a few material things."

Together they got the woman off the floor and into the nearby wingback chair.

"Would you take the guests – Bill included – into the dining room for wine and cheese, please? I want to talk to Mrs. Bell in private."

"Sure. Come this way everyone," Alain walked out the door waving his hand in the air beckoning the others to follow.

Alone with Eunice in the fireplace room, Jessica pulled a footstool over to the chair and sat down. "What frightened you so badly?"

"Oh I'm just being silly. A silly old woman."

"You're not silly and you're not old. Please, I want to know."

Mrs. Bell leaned forward in the chair. "I saw a man standing by the fireplace. But he wasn't one of your guests. I don't know who he was. He was transparent. He stood in front of you but I could see you through him. Oh, I'm not making any sense," she sighed.

"You're making perfect sense. I saw that man, too. When you screamed, I turned around and watched him glide across the room. He disappeared into the wall over there." Jessica pointed to the secret passage. "I don't mean to frighten you, but I think you – and I – we saw the ghost of Asher Hargrave."

"You mean the rumours about this place are true? That Hillcrest House really is haunted? Impossible."

Jessica pulled the footstool even closer to Eunice and took the woman's hand. "I don't think the Hargraves ever left here. I've heard children's laughter coming from the room over the kitchen. I've heard a woman crying. I saw footprints in the dust on the attic floor."

Mrs. Bell shook her head. "No, it can't be," she whispered. "There is no such thing as ghosts."

Alain stepped into the room. He sat a cup and saucer on the side table. "Here you go, Mrs. B. I made you some tea."

"Thank you, Const … I mean, Alain."

"No problem. You sit in here with Jess and rest."

"I think I'd rather go home. I'm sorry but this evening's events have upset me something awful," she dabbed at her chest with a napkin as she spoke.

"We'll find Bill and get him to take you home." Jessica stood to leave.

Eunice reached out and grabbed her arm. "Please, I don't want to be alone in here. What if he comes back?"

"Okay. I'll stay." She looked at Alain. "Will you find him, please and let him know that Mrs. Bell wants to leave?"

When he left the fireplace room, Jessica returned to the footstool. She took one of Eunice's hands in hers and stroked the back of it. The smell of smoke grew stronger and the room filled with the haze. She thought something blocked the flue but the smoke wasn't originating at the fireplace. It came from the other side of the room. The same ghost that appeared earlier, materialized through the wall. It glided to its place at the hearth and took a long draw on a pipe. It was tobacco smoke not wood smoke filling the room.

Alain returned with Mr. Bell. The cloud had vanished along with the odour. “Here he is, Mrs. B.”

Bill glowered at his wife but helped her out of the chair. Jessica walked them to the front door and bade them both a goodnight.

After she closed it behind the Bells, she leaned against the wall and sighed. Why was this ghost, if that’s what it was; only making himself visible to the two of them? Alain took her in his arms, kissed her forehead and held her close.

“Everyone is in the dining room. Let’s not keep them waiting any longer.” He broke the embrace and walked Jessica to the others, his arm around her waist.

“The missus wants to see the rest of the house,” the glazier piped up.

His wife, embarrassed, slapped his arm. “Oh Art.”

“Well if everyone is up for a tour, I’d love to show off what I’ve done with Hillcrest House.”

Jessica led the way through the pocket doors into the adjoining sitting room. “Since I first discovered the house online, I thought this was a woman’s sitting room. Softer furniture and colours in here as opposed to the fireplace room which I think is masculine in nature.”

Alain joined her at the head of the queue and the group ascended the stairs. The first room Jessica showed off on this floor was the one she had taken for her bedroom. The one that had the door to the balcony and bay window looking out over the clifftop. “I’ve rearranged the furniture in here. I like having the bed here so when I wake up in the morning, I can look straight out the windows. I found a box in the wardrobe with newspaper clippings about the Hargrave family. There are other papers and objects in it but I’ve not had the time to look at everything yet. I think the furniture in here looks feminine. Softer lines and curves. You’ll see what I mean a bit further on.”

The tour continued through the room over the kitchen where the peals of children’s laughter sometimes emanated. Not that she planned to have any more children, but Jessica left it as a nursery.

When she opened the door to the chamber above the fireplace room, an icy blast of air met her. She'd experienced this bone-chilling cold before in the house but not in this room. She checked the radiator and it was hot so the boiler hadn't quit. The rest of the house was comfortable, warm enough to wear a sleeveless dress and not have goosebumps. "Sorry about this room, folks. It's a bit nippy. Not sure if the heating system is working right or not." Did she tell her guests about the secret passage leading to the room below? So far, she hadn't discovered how to access it from in here. In the end, she decided against it. The location would remain undisclosed to her guests. Only she and Alain would know of its existence – aside from the ghost she'd seen pass through the wall into the cavity earlier. "When you compare the furnishings in here, they're bigger and chunkier than in my room which is why I believe this was once home to a man."

Jessica ushered everyone out of the room apologizing again for the numbing temperature. As she reached for the door, it slammed shut, shaking the house to the foundations. "Anyone interested in seeing the attic?"

A couple of the women declined but the others seemed content to continue the tour.

"Feel free to return to the dining room and help yourself to more wine and nibbles. We won't be too long." Jessica rubbed her hands up and down her arms trying to eliminate the chill that penetrated her to the bone.

Opening the door to the stairs to the next level, Jessica stepped aside. She allowed the others to go ahead of her with Alain taking the lead. She brought up the rear.

The temperature had returned to normal. Women who had slipped their sweaters on after the secret passage room now removed them.

As Jessica turned to lead the way towards the turret, she gasped in horror. The transparent figure of a woman glided through the door to the widow's walk and disappeared in the narrow passage.

She hoped no one else saw the apparition. It had only been she and Mrs. Bell who had seen the other specter downstairs.

She drew in a deep breath. “Over here in the turret is my office. Seems a bit strange to put it up here with the kitchen being two floors away and the bathroom one. But the views are spectacular which make up for the inconvenience.”

With the attic level opened up so that it was just one huge space, the light levels on the other side of the room improved.

“Well folks, this concludes the fifty-cent tour of Hillcrest House. There’s plenty to eat and drink in the dining room so shall we go back downstairs?” Jessica herded the guests towards the stairs but some continued milling about in the huge expanse of the room.

***

Jessica leaned back against the front door and sighed. The wine and cheese party had gone well except for she and Mrs. Bell seeing the ghost of Asher Hargrave. The neighbours’ curiosity had been sated. Maybe now, she could move on and live a normal life here in Angel Falls.

The dishes could wait until morning but she had to put the food away rather than leave it out and attract mice. She hadn’t seen any trace of them in months and didn’t want to tempt fate. Despite exhaustion she’d put the cheese and crackers away tonight.

When Jessica entered the dining room, Alain had cleared away the empty glasses and plates. He was taking platters of cheese and crackers back to the kitchen. It was a joy to watch him work. He appeared to be at home puttering in the kitchen. Her ex-husband never even offered to help out, let alone take the initiative. She joined Alain, wrapped leftover cheese for the fridge, and returned crackers to their packaging and the cupboards. “I’m going to make coffee. Do you want some?”

He checked his watch. “Sure but I’ll have to go as soon as it’s gone. I’m on duty – early shift – tomorrow.”

Jessica took mugs out of the upper cabinet and two pods from the carousel. She brewed them each a cup at a time in her Keurig. While the second one brewed, a huge blue light blasted out of the receptacle plunging the room into darkness. Sparks continued to flicker.

When Alain reached for the appliance's cord, she screamed, "Don't do it. You'll get electrocuted."

He pulled the plug anyway. "I'll go re-set the breaker."

The outlet sizzled and the last vestiges of the light show stopped. Jessica trembled. She had never had anything like this happen to her before.

"Flashlight. I'll need one."

With shaking hands, she rummaged in her junk drawer and pulled out her Maglite. "Th-the basement entrance is outside."

"I'll find it. Key. I trust you keep it locked."

Pointing to the hook by the back door, Jessica collapsed at the kitchen table. The house was finally finished the way she wanted. It could have all gone up in smoke. Once she regained her composure, she would call the electrician and give him a piece of her mind. It had to be something he'd done – or not done – that caused this to happen.

***

Alain grabbed Jessica's keys and made his way to the front door. The breaker had to be the issue. The only room affected was the kitchen. But, the lights and an outlet on the same one? That didn't seem right to him.

When he found the outside entrance to the basement, he held the flashlight between his chin and his chest with the beam shining on the door. He juggled the keys in one hand trying to find the right one and held the padlock in the other.

Lifting the one side of the hatch, he heaved it over until it lay flat away from the narrow steps. He didn't expect a light switch out here because of the possibility of water seeping in around the edges.

He shone the light down the half dozen or so steps and followed it to another door. Trying the knob, he discovered that this one wasn't secured. Alain pushed it open with his shoulder. The hinges creaked.

You couldn't consider this part of the house a basement. Cold, damp, dark cellar was more appropriate. There wasn't even a cement floor down here. It was dirt. Finding the light switch, he flicked it on.

A couple of bare bulbs hung down from the beams casting exaggerated shadows of the objects in the room. Even his shadow appeared distorted. The boiler and water heater sat on cement patio stones in the middle of the room between where he stood and the electrical panel mounted on the far wall.

Working his way around the space, Alain reached the breaker box. He shone the beam of the flashlight on each individual breaker. Not one had tripped. With the light show upstairs, that made no sense at all. He checked them all again with the same result. He thought for sure that a breaker had blown.

Satisfied that everything down here was safe, he returned to the entrance, turned out the lights and secured the basement inside and out.

When Alain walked in the front door, he heard Jessica's voice. She sounded angry. He continued through to the kitchen.

"I paid you good money to re-wire this house and I expect it done properly. Flames shooting out of an outlet doesn't sound like you did it the way it should have been done."

There was a lull in the conversation. Alain assumed the person on the other end was speaking.

"No I haven't checked the breakers, yet."

Alain grabbed the phone away from her. "She didn't. I did. Not a single one tripped."

"I know I did everything right. Lightning Electrical stands behind their work and on their good reputation."

"Steve. I might have known. I don't care that it's going on midnight. I want you over here tonight and this mess cleared up."

"But…"

"No buts."

"If you'd let me finish. Maybe the cord's frayed or shorting out at the plug."

"There was nothing wrong with it," Alain growled. He detested Steve under normal circumstances. This was far from normal.

Disconnecting the call, he paced from one end of the kitchen to the other. The electrician had been the reason he lost the first woman he loved. He wasn't going to be responsible for the loss of another.

He had said that *L* word again when referring to Jessica. Maybe his feelings did go much deeper than he had admitted to himself all this time. He knew he cared for her and enjoyed her company. But did he love her? Could he let go of the past?

22

Steve arrived at Hillcrest House within the hour. He checked the Keurig's cord and plug before disappearing into the cellar.

"I don't like the way he treats you," Alain grumbled.

"What do you mean?" Jessica looked up from the napkin she'd ripped to pieces.

"Like you're a helpless woman who doesn't know anything."

"I think you're exaggerating," she replied sweeping the remnants of the serviette into her hand.

Before Alain had a chance to answer, the electrician reappeared in the doorway. "I've shut the power off to this breaker." He took a screwdriver out of his toolbox. "I'll replace the outlet and see if that makes any difference."

"Okay," she nodded.

Steve no sooner touched the screw holding the cover in place when a blue flash followed by a loud bang came from the receptacle. It knocked him backwards across the room.

Jessica clapped her hand over her mouth. She knew enough about electricity to know that if the breaker was off, he wouldn't have been on the receiving end of an electrical shock. "Are-are you all right?" she stammered crouching beside him.

"You turned the right breaker off?" Alain jibed.

"Of course I turned the right breaker off. I wired this place, labelled the panel. I know what breaker is what."

"All right you two. Enough." She yanked the screwdriver out of Steve's hand, walked to the outlet and removed the cover without incident.

Things were getting too freaky. Steve almost got electrocuted but she used his screwdriver to do the same thing and nothing happened? In the beginning, she hadn't believed the stories about Hillcrest House. After hearing children laughing in the room above the kitchen and a woman crying she began to have doubts. She saw the ghost of a man in the fireplace room. A room that later filled with smoke and smelled of the aroma of burning pipe tobacco. Those weren't normal every day occurrences.

Steve finished the task without further mishap. When he returned from the cellar after turning the breaker back on, his face had lost all colour. "I swear I turned the breaker off, but when I got to the panel, it was on." He scratched his head. "I don't get it."

"I'll see you to the door when you're ready," Jessica offered.

Alain scowled at her.

She didn't care if being courteous to the electrician bothered Alain. It was her house, her electrical problem.

***

"Shall we try this again?" Jessica asked when she returned from seeing Steve out.

"I really wish you hadn't hired him in the first place," Alain grumbled. "I hate the thought of him being under the same roof as you."

He sounded like he was jealous on top of his hatred for the man. He had nothing to worry about on that front. Mr. Lightning Electrical wasn't her type. Unless he overpowered her, which seemed doubtful, he would be the last person she wanted sharing her bed. Second last – her ex-husband remained at the top of the list.

"The fire is still burning. I hate to put it out. I'll make us some more coffee and we'll go sit in there."

"How about this instead?" He produced a bottle of Armagnac and two tulip-shaped snifters. "I think we deserve something stronger, don't you?"

23

Jessica wet her lips in anticipation as Alain stirred the fire with the brass poker and added another log. His snug trousers clung to his firm butt. He was so fit, not to mention French making her wonder if what they said about lovers of that nationality was true. Were they the best? She'd be a guinea pig and test the theory. Soon the flames danced and crackled and he joined her on the sofa.

The events of the evening after the guests had gone left her chilled. She snuggled closer to Alain to soak up some of the body heat radiating off him. Feeling daring, and perhaps a bit brazen, she lifted his right arm over her and cuddled closer. His fingertips brushed against her nipple through the silky fabric of her dress and lace bra. It stiffened at the caress and her breath quickened.

Alain placed his snifter on the end table. He took Jessica's glass from her and sat it alongside his. He cupped her cheek in his left hand and kissed her on the lips. His tongue worked its way into her mouth. He tasted of the Armagnac.

Without breaking their embrace, Alain lifted Jessica from the couch and laid her on the floor in front of it. He slid his hand up her thigh under her dress and over the lacy fabric of her panties covering her bum. She moaned and rolled onto her back.

When he placed his hand on her flat bare stomach, something slimy dripped onto Jessica's bare arm. She glanced at the spot. It looked like blood. She pulled back from Alain and cast her eyes towards the ceiling at an expanding red, wet patch.

Jessica scrambled up from the floor. The stench from whatever oozed down from above made her sick. She raced from the room holding her hand over her mouth, out the front door, and into the yard where she threw up.

***

Alain wasn't far behind. He recognized the putrid odour. Taking deep breaths through his nose to banish the smell from his nostrils, he pulled out his BlackBerry and called the station. Jessica was on her hands and knees retching when he reached her side. "They're sending … a forensics … team," he blurted out as his chest heaved trying to get fresh air into his lungs.

He crouched beside her and rubbed her back before helping her to her feet and away from her vomit. "Do you want to go to the kitchen and get some water?"

"No. I don't ever want to go in that place again," she shrieked and pushed him away.

"Do you want me to go in and get you something?"

"D-do you mind? I need to get this awful taste out of my mouth. I had a package of Scotch mints in the drawer by the sink."

"No problem." Alain walked her to the verandah and helped her sit before entering the mansion.

The front door remained open from when they dashed out to escape the slime and offensive smell. The foul odour had started to dissipate. Not wanting to linger longer than necessary, Alain sprinted to the kitchen and found the package of peppermint candies.

"Here you go," he sighed and handed the bag to Jessica.

She removed one and sucked on it before giving the cellophane bag back. He popped two into his mouth and breathed in. The fresh scent replaced the nasty one from earlier.

The black SUV pulled around the corner and two officers stepped out. Alain strode over to brief them on the events.

White boiler suits donned, the police followed him to the front door. As they stepped over the threshold, they pulled out blue paper booties and placed them over their shoes. Alain pointed to the room where the incident took place.

Jessica shivered. He put his arm around her and pulled her

close. "Are you sure you don't want to go inside? You're freezing."

She shook her head, grabbed the front of his shirt and clung to it then buried her face in his chest.

"At least let me get you a coat."

Jessica gripped his clothing tighter. He pried her hands off and stood up. He had hung his coat inside the front door when he arrived earlier in the evening. He could grab it and not compromise the investigation.

Returning with the garment, he draped it over Jessica's shoulders before resuming his position beside her. He looked skyward and pulled Jessica closer to him. None of it made sense.

Alain knew strange things happened at Hillcrest House but he tried to look at them logically. The episode with the crow flying at the window – simple, it saw its reflection and thought it was another crow. But that didn't completely wash because crows are gregarious. Tonight in the kitchen – an electrical fault due to shoddy workmanship. That didn't explain no tripped breakers when he went to the basement to check. And if Steve did turn the one off to the outlet in the kitchen, then it shouldn't have blown him across the room. But Jessica took the cover off and she was fine.

Had an animal got trapped in the house when it crawled between the joists? It could be a cat or squirrel. It could have happened before Jessica arrived. There would be plenty of time for decomp to begin and be at the black putrefaction stage now. That was the only logical explanation.

"Hey, Alain, can you come in here?" Jake yelled from the fireplace room.

"I better go see what he wants. You be okay out here on your own?"

She nodded. "Go on."

Alain got to his feet and went back inside the house. "Yeah, what?"

"Where exactly was this ooze dripping from?"

He pointed to a spot straight above the place on the floor where he and Jessica had lain.

"You're sure."

"Of course I'm sure. What do you take me for?"

"Then how do you explain the ceiling being completely dry," Jake scoffed.

"What do you mean?"

"Look! See for yourself."

Sure enough, the ceiling was dry – not even stained. What the hell? Things were getting way too weird for his liking.

Gus climbed down from the ladder. "Nothing there, mate. You sure you and your lady friend aren't imagining it?"

"Yes."

"Well, there's nothing up there but a recently painted ceiling. Might as well pack …," he paused sniffing the air. "Okay that smell wasn't there a few minutes ago."

The foul odour reached Alain's nose and caught in the back of his throat. At least now, he felt vindicated. The stench started like it was off in the distance but grew stronger. Gus and Jake worked their way around the room trying to find its source.

"It's coming from behind this wall," Gus stated. He stood in front of the section where the panelling went all the way to the ceiling.

Alain started across the room.

"You stay where you are, Fournier," Jake barked. "Don't need you contaminating the scene." After ordering Alain to stay put, he joined the other cop. The two spoke in hushed tones so not to be overheard. "Aw-yup, we're going to have to tear this piece of wall out."

"No!" Jessica shrieked.

Alain spun around. He reached out and drew her to his side.

"If you want to get rid of the smell, we've got to get behind the wall," Jake reiterated.

"Absolutely not," she snapped. Jessica walked to the fireplace, pulled on the ring in the evil looking sculpture's mouth, and turned it.

The section of the wall the forensics team wanted to destroy opened. The sickening stench enveloped the room.

Jake and Gus took flashlights out of their belts and disappeared into the hidden cavity.

As much as Alain wanted to find the source of the smell, he was useless to the investigation. He needed a boiler suit, paper booties and at least one pair of nitrile gloves. Sure, the guys had extras in the vehicle but they'd claim he was too close to the situation. Despite being uncomfortable in his *civilian* role, he took Jessica out to the kitchen. "They're going to find the source of that stink and get rid of it," he soothed. "They're not going to destroy anything. I won't let them."

"Why me?" she moaned.

"I can't answer that." He leaned over and kissed the top of her head. "You stay here. I'm going to see if they've made any progress."

***

When Alain reached the entrance to the fireplace room, the forensics team was packing up.

"Bugger me, didn't find a damn thing," Jake grumbled. "I don't get it. With the smell I would have expected a large corpse."

Gus rooted in his kit and pulled out a couple of pouches. "Here, just in case it comes back. This should neutralize the smell." He tossed them to Alain. "I'll be jiggered with this one. The stink was definitely in the room. That's not something you can recreate. What I don't get is why it was so strong when we first arrived and then pretty much dissipated before coming back. We should have found a body. Even if it was just a good sized rodent."

After the investigators left, Alain opened one of the pouches. He placed it on the end table beneath the location on the ceiling from where the dark slime had dripped. Retrieving the glasses and bottle of Armagnac, he took them through to the kitchen and dumped the open drinks down the sink.

***

When Jessica heard water running she looked up. Relieved it was Alain rinsing their snifters and not some other fault with the house she bowed her head. More problems with Hillcrest House were the last thing she wanted or needed. She didn't know if she wanted to spend another night under the same roof as the ghosts and other unexplained phenomena.

Despite having Alain's jacket wrapped around her shoulders, she shivered from the cold. He was in shirtsleeves and didn't seem to mind the temperature. Maybe that's why the terrible odour hadn't appeared before tonight. It could have been the heat from having everyone in the room and the fireplace lit. The room had gotten rather warm. The rise in temperature could have brought it back from wherever it had lingered in obscurity. The only thing she knew was she didn't want to spend the night in the house.

Alain sat down beside her and took both of her hands in his. She loved the feel of his skin on hers – smooth and soft, yet masculine. Tears pricked at the backs of her eyes. She was going to cry again and didn't want to do it in front of him. Blinking hard, she forced her tears back. "I don't want to stay here," she whispered.

"Do you want to go to the Bells? I'll take you there. I'm sure they would be happy to let you spend the night."

"Not at this hour. I don't want to wake them. Besides, Mrs. Bell had enough excitement earlier this evening, thanks to the ghost of Asher Hargrave."

He hadn't jumped at the opportunity to take her back to his place where they could finish what they had started earlier. Did he not want to make love to her? She wanted him to. "I need you. Can't we go to your place? We're both wide awake." She tried appealing to his logical side and hoped he'd take the not-so-subtle hint.

***

Alain raked his hand over his shaved head. She looked vulnerable leaning on the table in her blue satin cocktail dress with his leather jacket around her shoulders. Would he be taking advantage of her if they went back to his place? Still, things might have progressed further had something not driven them from in front of the roaring fire.

"I'll go check and make sure we're not going to set the house ablaze while you throw what you need for overnight in a bag," he said helping her up from the table. When Jessica was on her feet, he pulled her close to him. She smelled damn good – a combination of her perfume and his leather coat. His self-imposed celibacy would end that night.

Before he let her go, he leaned down to kiss her but she pulled away.

"You don't want to do that," she blurted out. "I mean, I have barf breath."

He chuckled and put his arm around her shoulder. They walked out into the hallway where they parted company at the foot of the stairs.

The fireplace room was dark except for the glow of a few embers on the grate. Alain moved the heavy screen onto the hearth to prevent any sparks from getting through. Satisfied that it would be safe for the night, he walked to the front door to wait for Jessica.

When she appeared at the top of the stairs, she hadn't changed her clothes. He wanted to be the one to undress her and would have done so earlier in the evening if not for the unplanned disruption.

24

Jessica accepted Alain's hand. He helped her out of the car and leaned her against the rear passenger door. She shivered with excitement when he ran his fingers down the side of her face and neck. When their lips met, she eagerly opened her mouth and found his tongue.

He put his hands inside the jacket and cupped her breasts. Her nipples rose to attention at his touch. Kissing his way over her cheek, down her neck and into the plunging neckline of her dress caused her knees to weaken.

Alain scooped her up into his arms, and grabbed her overnight bag. He carried her to the entrance. The building appeared modern. A few units were still illuminated but most were in darkness. Jessica wondered which one he lived in.

When they reached the main entrance, he pushed the handicapped access button and carried her through the opening and into a waiting elevator. There were mirrors on the interior walls above the handrails. Jessica wished he'd balance her on them in one of the corners and make love to her right then and there. She nuzzled her face into the side of his neck and kissed it. Grabbed his tight ass and pulled his hips into her. Oh God, she wanted him so bad.

After what seemed like an eternity, the lift stopped and the doors opened. The corridor on this floor screamed money and lots of it. It seemed far too opulent for a police officer's salary. Maybe it wasn't an apartment or condominium complex but a luxury hotel. It didn't matter to Jessica as long as she was with Alain.

He set her down and unlocked the door then kicked it closed behind them.

Once inside, he cupped her face in his hands and kissed her hungrily. Lips locked together, they staggered towards the living room, bumping off walls and tearing at each other's clothes. Jessica tugged at his shirt to untuck it from his trousers but they were too tight. She fumbled with his belt to unbuckle it.

Before she had the chance to do any more, Alain stopped and held her at arm's length. Had she done something wrong? Was he not as ready to move on as he claimed to be? She needn't have worried. He slid her arms out of his leather jacket and tossed it onto the sofa. Chills of excitement coursed through her veins fanning the fire between her legs.

Reaching around behind her, Alain found the tab and pulled down the zipper of her dress. Kissing her neck, he peeled the straps off her shoulders. The slippery fabric slid down her arms and into a pool of blue satin on the floor leaving her in just her bra, panties and high heels. He kissed and nibbled his way down her neck to her chest. Slipped his hand inside her bra and cupped her breast pushing the lacy fabric out of the way. His hot, moist breath on her bare skin drove her insane with desire. He took her breast in his mouth swirling his tongue around her nipple before turning his attention to the other one and working his way down to the top of her lace panties.

Jessica yanked his shirttails out of his pants and unbuttoned the garment. When it hung open, she wrapped her arms around his firm, muscular body and wrapped one leg around him, pulling him closer.

Kissing her bare shoulder, Alain unfastened her bra and removed it before picking her up and carrying her to the bedroom. He laid her on the duvet. "You're beautiful," he whispered, his voice husky with desire as he climbed onto the bed between her legs. He leaned over her and kissed her.

Hooking his thumbs into the waistband of her panties, he rolled them down her body and dropped them onto the floor. He removed his shirt and threw it aside before undoing his trousers and slipping them and his boxer briefs off.

He traced up her body with the tip of his tongue. Jessica squirmed at his touch. He dipped his hand between her legs and suckled her breast. A low moan escaped from her lips. His touch drove her mad with desire. One finger, then two found their way into her silky wetness taking her to the brink. His thumb found her secret spot. Within seconds of his touch, she exploded in a flash of passion – her muscles contracting around his fingers.

Alain crushed his mouth on hers, kissing her with a desire she had never experienced. She opened her mouth to receive his tongue and at the same time, he pushed his hardened member into her. Breath coming in short gasps; Jessica arched her back and raised her hips to accept him.

Wrapping her legs around him, she met his thrusts with a fervor she had forgotten existed within her. He brought her to the brink then slowed his rhythmic movements before speeding up again. When she climaxed, he pushed deep into her one last time.

They lay together sweaty and spent. When Alain rolled onto his back, Jessica cuddled to him. She fell asleep wrapped in his arms.

25

The shrill ringtone of her cell phone jolted Jessica awake. Where was she? This wasn't her room at Hillcrest House. Beside her, snuggled under the duvet, lay Alain. She lifted the down-filled blanket and peered beneath it. She hadn't dreamt the events from the previous night. Early this morning would be more appropriate. They hadn't left Hillcrest House until after one o'clock. Fumbling on the nightstand, she found the irritating device and pressed the talk button. "Hello." No one replied. She ended the call then checked the callers list. No new ones. That made no sense. The thing rang long enough that it should have registered.

Jessica slipped out of bed and grabbed Alain's shirt from its resting place. Shrugging her arms into the sleeves, she climbed out of bed and walked to the window. She opened the drawn curtains a crack to see what it was like outdoors and get an idea of where she was. Tiptoeing out of the room, she left Alain sleeping and entered the huge living room.

When they came in during the wee hours of the morning, passion consumed her rather than his decorating tastes. Chunky, black leather sofa, smoky glass topped coffee table and end tables and a huge flat-screen TV mounted on the white wall on the opposite side of the room. No colour accents of any kind – just black and white. Even the heavy, floor-length, grommet curtain panels were black.

Jessica found her overnight bag and pulled a pair of sport socks from it. After putting them on, she padded over to the drapes and pushed them aside. French doors led out onto a balcony. She unlocked the doors, pulled them open towards her, and stepped out. The view from here was almost as good as from the widow's walk on Hillcrest House. There were no terraces above her, so Alain's apartment was on the top.

26

On the way back to Hillcrest House later that day, Alain tried to reassure Jessica that everything would be fine. Yesterday's events were a one off – a fluke. He hated having to leave her there alone but he had to work. At least with his job, he could drive by at random intervals and check on her. Although not a perfect solution, it did give him some comfort.

Pulling his black Charger into the driveway, he brought it to a stop beside her little Aveo. After he turned the ignition off, he turned to her. "I'm only a phone call away. You know that."

She nodded.

"I'll come in with you, or go ahead of you even, if that's what you'd like and make sure everything is okay."

"Please."

Alain got out of the car, came around to the passenger side and helped Jessica out. He grabbed her bag off the backseat, and put his arm around her. The closer they got to the front door, the more she resisted.

"I don't want to go in. What if it starts all over again?" she moaned.

"It will be fine. I'm sure."

A crow cawed and swooped down to the verandah railing. When Alain saw the lone white feather in its neck, he recognized the bird right away. "Go on. Get out of here," he shouted.

To his horror, Jessica extended her arm and it flew to her and landed on her outstretched limb. It bobbed its head up and down and squawked a few times.

Positive the bird was mocking him, he stared it down hoping it would leave. Instead, the crow held its ground and glared back at him through its shiny, black eyes.

Wrestling the keys out of Jessica's hand, he unlocked the front door. Manners dictated that he let her enter first, but given her frame of mind, he elected to go in ahead of her. Once he crossed the threshold, he extended his arm and took her hand. The crow hopped off and continued across the verandah, all the while not taking its eyes off him.

Alain eased Jessica into the foyer a bit at a time. It was hard because she could be stubborn and this was one of those times.

The smell that drove them out of the house had dissipated to the point it was no longer detectable. He stepped into the fireplace room. The stain on the ceiling remained invisible, like it had never been there.

He drew Jessica close to him and stood with his arm around her in the doorway to the room where the events unfolded. "See, I told you it would be okay."

With a blank stare, she nodded.

"I'll take your bag upstairs and check the rest of the house."

***

Jessica watched Alain take the stairs two at a time. His footsteps on the hardwood floors above echoed through the quiet house. At least things seemed back to normal. It wouldn't be completely so living in this old Victorian mansion with a crow for a pet, and a cop for a boyfriend. He was her boyfriend, wasn't he? They had slept together. She hoped she wasn't just another notch on his bedpost. She had never been a one-night stand before and didn't fancy becoming one now.

She wandered down the corridor to the kitchen. When she reached the doorway, voices shouting at each other, filled the air. One was definitely a man; the other a woman. Did she come home in the middle of a domestic between Asher and Maggie Hargrave?

Concentrating to try to make out the words, Jessica didn't hear Alain come into the room.

"I've got to run," he whispered.

Startled, she jumped. "You scared the life out of me," she scolded.

"I'm sorry. I'll check in on you later." He kissed her forehead and left.

Alain didn't tell her if everything checked out all right upstairs. She assumed if it hadn't, he would have said something. Sighing, Jessica took a mug out of the cupboard and turned on her Keurig. It came on without any problems. No blue sparks. No electrical current shooting her across the room like what happened to the electrician. While waiting for it to preheat, she chose the blend she wanted and leaned against the counter.

Drink in hand, she climbed the stairs to her office in the turret and turned on her laptop. When it booted up, she opened her email. A couple of new ones from people wanting custom book covers were waiting in her inbox. She opened the first one. At least the sender adhered to her guidelines. She printed the email and took it over to her drafting table. As she assembled her pencils, erasers and shields, she read the message again. Jessica formulated a concept in her mind before pinning the sheet of paper to the corkboard on the wall. She liked working this way. She could start on the computer straight off but preferred to let the image flow onto paper from her mind first. Once she and the client had agreed on the cover image, only then did she do the finish work on the computer.

She began the preliminary sketch. Unhappy with it, she crumpled the paper and tossed it in the waste paper basket. Starting again, she still couldn't get the concept drawn. After half a dozen aborted attempts, Jessica called it quits. When she found herself in these funks, it was better to stop and do something else for a while.

Undecided on what she could do to clear her mind, Jessica went downstairs to her room. Her holdall that she'd taken with her to Alain's the night before – or was it the same day, just in the wee hours of the morning – sat on the bed. She unpacked it then remembered the wooden box in the top of the wardrobe. Maybe she could concentrate on going through that. Moving the dressing table stool into position, she climbed up on it and removed the chest.

27

Jessica placed the wooden box on the side table next to the wingback chair by the window in the parlour. She did not intend to return to the fireplace room any time soon. Wrapping a throw around her, she made herself comfortable and placed the coffer on her lap.

She lifted the lid revealing the contents. The top article covered Asher's death at the sawmill. She had read it when she first found the chest so set it aside. Something about that piece reminded her of the one she found in the sideboard in the dining room behind her.

Returning the box to the table, Jessica stood. The pocket doors that separated the two rooms were wide open. She liked it that way. The dining room had a beautiful bay window letting in lots of light. In turn, the sitting room was brighter, too. She found the clipping in the drawer where she'd put it before the wine and cheese party cum open house.

Loud cawing made her look up and outside. The crow – her crow – perched on the verandah railing with something in its talons. From where she stood, it appeared to be paper or maybe the remnants of a shopping bag. Curious about what the bird had brought this time, she went outside to investigate. When she took it, the crow squawked and bobbed its head up and down. The texture of the object was wrong for paper or plastic. It was filthy whatever it was. Rubbing it between her thumb and forefinger, it felt like fabric of some kind. It would need cleaning before she could tell.

***

In the kitchen, Jessica turned on the cold water and held

the gift from the crow under the flow from the tap. The dirt created a dark brown almost black stream under it. She squeezed some dishwashing liquid onto the piece of material and worked it in before scrubbing. The water flowing from it now was sudsy and grey. At least she had made a start at cleaning it. Rinsing it well, she repeated the process. After the fourth sequence, Jessica had removed enough dirt to make a determination. It looked like a small scrap of tweed. Still, she had no idea where the crow had found it. She squeezed as much water out of it as possible then wrapped it in paper towelling to soak up the rest.

After drying her hands, she returned to the dining room and retrieved the clipping she had left on the table. When Jessica picked up the article, she recognized the scrap of material as the same as from the photo in the newspaper clipping. Stunned by the similarity, her jaw dropped. Was her latest gift from the crow a piece of Lucille Walker's clothing from the picture? If so, how did the bird get it? Chills ran up her spine and she shivered.

28

Jessica rushed back to the kitchen and unwrapped the fabric from the paper towelling. There was no mistaking it. The piece of cloth and the pattern in the picture were a perfect match, even though the quality of images in old newspapers was far from perfect.

Returning to her sitting room, she got comfortable in her chair again. Jessica placed the coffer in her lap and laid the piece of material and newspaper clipping on the side table. The next article was about Maggie's death and then obituaries documenting the deaths of the Hargrave children. Their family history was tragic. The fact that one child had died from the same cause as her own, shook Jessica to the core. She pulled out another yellowed article and read.

Angel Falls Freeholder July 30, 1905

CHILDEN OF PROMINENT LOCAL SAW MILL OWNER DROWN IN RIVER NEAR THE BASE OF ANGEL FALLS

The drowning of Asher Hargrave's two eldest children, thirteen year-old twins Charles and Elizabeth, near the base of Angel Falls occurred yesterday. When help arrived, the domestic employed by the family was frantically trying to revive them. Tragically, it was not to be.

Mother, Maggie Hargrave, collapsed on the lifeless bodies wailing in a fit of despair. She had been at the family home at the time of the mishap and brought to the scene by a member of the local constabulary.

Mr. Hargrave arrived soon after authorities notified him at work. Witnesses say he appeared more shaken and embarrassed by his wife's actions than the deaths of his children.

A tear ran down Jessica's cheek and she swiped it away with the back of her hand. What sort of family were the Hargraves? The husband more upset by his wife's behaviour than the deaths of his children. She took a few deep breaths to compose herself. Reading the obituaries of the children and now this newspaper account of the drowning, saddened her.

Setting the last clipping aside, Jessica reached into the coffer and took out a packet of letters bound with a pink, satin ribbon.

Untying the knot and letting the silky fabric slip away, she took the envelope from the top of the stack and pulled the letter out. She began to read.

September 30, 1907

My dearest Asher,

Those moments we shared during your wife's stay in the insane asylum were the happiest ones I've had here at Hillcrest House in many years. It sounds selfish of me to say it, given you and she have lost all four of your children in tragic circumstances.

Now that Mrs. Hargrave is home, my loyalties have to be with her. I have to help her heal and get well again so that she can return to being the wife you once knew and loved in every way.

It will be difficult for me to hide my feelings for you and I'm hoping it will be for you as well. We can't continue to live as we have. Please, you must be strong for me so that I can get through this difficult situation. It would have been better had this never happened between us but it has and we must forget about it.

All my love always,

Lucille

Dumbfounded, she read the letter again. Lucille. Lucille. She was the domestic who had gone missing in the article Jessica discovered in the sideboard. The crow presented her with a scrap of fabric matching the clothing the young woman wore in the grainy photograph that accompanied the piece. Asher and Lucille had an affair.

October 5, 1907

Darling Lucille,

Please do not torture yourself over what has happened between us these last few years. I have never been so happy as I am when I'm with you. Even when I courted Maggie before we wed, I didn't feel this same way.

I don't know if I'll be able to do as you requested

in your letter but I shall do my best. If it weren't for Maggie and her health, I would divorce her so that I could spend the rest of my life with you.

I pledge my love forever,

Asher

That miserable git! Carrying on with the maid during the time his wife spent in an asylum. He should be strung up. Having an affair was bad enough. But after poor Maggie suffered from a nervous breakdown and packed off to the looney bin? What woman wouldn't go a bit mad after losing *all* her children?

Still, so intrigued by the letters, Jessica had to continue reading. She'd opened Pandora's box and there was no closing it.

October 10, 1907

My dearest Asher,

I don't know how to begin this letter. I certainly didn't mean to entrap you. However, I've been late with my courses and the doctor has confirmed that I am with child. I don't know what to do. I could never get rid of it knowing that you are the father.

Please help me.

All my love always,

Lucille

Jessica couldn't wait to tell Alain of her discovery. She looked at her cell phone and willed it to ring. Nothing happened. She didn't want to call him when he was working. He could be in the middle of something and not able to speak with her. Although anxious to share this motherlode of Hillcrest House history, it would have to keep until he checked in with her. She hoped it would be in person but a phone call would suffice.

October 15, 1907

Darling Lucille,

You don't know how happy your last letter has made me. I'm to be a father again. I'm giddy with the delight of knowing this joyous fact.

You could never entrap me. I love you far too much to ever feel that way about you.

Whatever you need, I will provide for you. I want to help you to raise our child, even if we can't be together. You only have to ask. Please remember that.

I pledge my love forever,

Asher

A lump formed in Jessica's throat. The side of Asher revealed in the letters between him and Lucille showed a tender, loving man. The exact opposite of the man who admonished his wife for making a scene when their oldest children died. He cared about this young girl and their love child.

May 17, 1908

My dearest Asher,

I've brought too much shame and scandal to your family. I miss you already and I've not even left Angel Falls yet.

I'm going away to have the baby. Our baby conceived out of the love we have for each other. I believe Mrs. Hargrave means to do me harm. Don't ask how I know. It's just a feeling I have deep inside me.

As much as it breaks my heart to say this, please don't look for me. It will be better that way.

All my love always,

Lucille

Pregnant and frightened, Lucille was running away. Not only that, being a single woman and in her condition was beyond reproach. Worse still, to be in that condition with her employer's child. Jessica expected the next letter to be from Asher since the previous ones all followed along in chronological order. Maybe he met her somewhere and tried to convince her to stay.

May 25, 1908

My dearest Asher,

I left the train at the next stop and have sought shelter at the convent. Your wife boarded the train.

She was in the next carriage. I saw her on the platform. She is following me. I'm even more convinced that she means to do me harm now. Why else would she get on the same train?

I hope I vanished into the crowd and escaped the station without her seeing.

The Mother Superior says I can stay here with the sisters until after the birth. I do hope it's soon. She will also look after seeing the child adopted like they did once before.

You see, when I was a young girl of about fourteen, I found myself with child. One of my father's associates forced himself upon me. My family didn't believe me when I told them what happened. They preferred to believe his side of the story. After all, he was a prominent businessman in the community. My parents said I shamed the family. They took me to the convent where I gave birth to a little girl. That's all the sisters told me and I had to plead with them to find out that much.

We never planned on me getting with child so this is the best solution for everyone. I know I could never raise the baby on my own knowing you are the father and that I would never see you again.

Please, don't be angry with me.

All my love always,

Lucille

29

Picking up the article covering Lucille's disappearance again, Jessica tried to do the math. Heavily pregnant meant the woman was about eight months along. She was likely about three months when she told Asher she was pregnant. There was a huge gap between letters and no replies from him. The two could have met many times between then and when Lucille said she was leaving.

When Jessica's cellphone rang, she jumped. Engrossed in the letters, she tried to put together the remaining pieces of the puzzle. "Alain," she exclaimed. Without giving him a chance to speak, she continued. "You wouldn't believe what I found. Can you come over? I need to show you."

"It's crazy here today. Seems every arsewipe and his brother are out on the roads. Not sure if I can get away or not but I did say I would check in and make sure you're okay. You might have to settle for this phone call."

Jessica's heart sank. She so wanted to see Alain and show him her discoveries. "What time are you off work," she asked trying not to sound disappointed.

"Shift ends at seven. Paperwork will take at least half an hour. Likely won't be able to get out of the detachment much before eight … that is, if I'm lucky."

"Come here when you get off work then. I'll make you a meal. And you can see everything I found today."

"I can do that," Alain agreed. After Jessica ended the call, she glanced at the clock. It was just past five. Now, what was she going to cook for them? Opening the fridge door, she peered in. Leftover cheese from her party. Not exciting but would make a nice snack before or after their meal with crackers. She didn't have time to go shopping. If she started now she'd be late back and wouldn't be able to serve more than biscuits and cheese.

The freezer! Jessica opened the lid on the chest unit and rummaged around. She found a lasagna she'd made and frozen a couple of weeks ago for just such an occasion and took it out. About the same time it would have to go into the oven, she would make a Caesar salad.

Jessica tidied up the sitting room where she had the newspaper clippings and love letters out. Once back in the same order as she read them, she returned them to the coffer. She would show Alain before they had their meal. Tonight was special. This was the first time she had actually cooked from scratch for him. They'd eaten together here at Hillcrest House before. They got a takeaway – Chinese, Indian or pizza. Now they had slept together for the first time so she needed to make everything perfect.

She closed the pocket doors separating the dining room and her sitting room. She set the table for two with her best china plates and crystal wine glasses. Thinking back, these were among the best things she got from her divorce settlement.

There was plenty of wine left over from the night before so it was just a matter of selecting the best one. The candles in her silver candlesticks were stubs. Jessica replaced them with fresh, stearin ones and set them between the place settings. Alain might not know it yet, but he was spending the night here with her.

Speaking of that, she needed a bath. Well, maybe not needed but wanted. After all, she had to look and smell her best for him. Another cursory glance at the clock and she climbed the stairs.

Turning on the tap, Jessica poured a generous dollop of vanilla bubble bath into the tub. As it filled, she undressed. Checking the temperature of the water and deciding it was fine, she climbed in. She allowed the tub to fill until it was about six inches from the top. When it reached the desired depth, she turned off the faucet and settled into the luxurious foamy water.

Suddenly, pressure on her shoulders pushed her under the water and held her there. Jessica gasped for air and swallowed a mouthful of the scented bath. Sputtering when she got her head above water, she reached ready to dig her fingernails in to her unknown assailant's hands. There was nothing there but empty air. No arms, no hands, no person, nothing. She fumbled for the edges of the tub while she continued fighting her attacker. Jessica squirmed and kicked, and rammed the big toe on her right foot into the spout. For a moment she forgot about fighting – the pain overrode her survival instinct. Once she quit trying to prevent herself from drowning, the weight on her body disappeared and she could move again.

Jessica scrambled out of the tub, grabbed the chain for the plug and gave it a tug. A loud sucking noise filled the room as the water whirlpooled down the drain. The room was freezing cold. She could see her breath. She pulled her huge bath sheet off the heated towel rack. The words *you'll be the next to die* appeared in the frost on the mirror. Wrapping the cover around her, she fled.

When Jessica reached her room, she slammed the door behind her and leaned against it. She remained in that position until her breathing slowed and her chest quit heaving. Using the skeleton key she kept in the keyhole on the interior side of the room, Jessica locked the door. It wouldn't be much of a deterrent to a ghost but even a false sense of security was better than none. The warmth from the heavy terrycloth surrounding her body soothed her.

The apparition that tried to drown her couldn't be Lucille. When she encountered her before the wine and cheese party, she seemed docile. No, it had to be Maggie. But why? Did the woman feel threatened by Jessica's presence in the house?

Opening her wardrobe doors, she studied the clothing hanging inside. She decided on her favourite skinny jeans even though Alain had seen her in them before. Jessica tossed them onto the bed. She took a black three-quarter length sleeve, cowl-neck pullover out of her highboy. It joined the pants along with a matching set of black lace bra and panties. She found a pair of no-show, black and red sport socks for her feet.

Dried, moisturized, and dressed, she sat down at her dressing table and applied her makeup. She didn't realize she had spent so long in the bath until the grandfather clock in the foyer chimed seven. Spraying some mousse into her hand, she raked her fingers through her hair and scrunched it.

***

Jessica poured a glass of red wine from one of the bottles opened the night before and turned the oven on to preheat. While she waited for it to finish, she removed the head of romaine from the crisper and washed it. She didn't use her wooden salad bowl and tongs often so had to scrounge in the cupboards for them.

Lettuce washed and spun, she tore it and dropped it into the bowl. She could make the dressing now and just wait until it was time to eat to pour it over the salad. Jessica returned the greens to the fridge so they didn't wilt. While she held the door open, Jessica took the jar of anchovy paste from its shelf. Olive oil and white balsamic vinegar were in the pantry. Lemons were in the ceramic fruit bowl she kept on her kitchen table.

She hummed while making the dressing. Three parts oil, two parts vinegar, a crushed clove of garlic, a smidgeon of the fish paste and a couple of grinds of pepper from her mill. Jessica combined the ingredients in a mason jar and set it in the refrigerator until later. Croutons and lemon juice would go in when it was time to serve the salad.

By now, the oven was hot and she put the lasagna in. It would take about an hour to cook. They would have a late supper around eight-thirty, providing Alain was able to get out of the police station at the planned time.

She closed the door that joined the kitchen and dining room. She wanted to surprise Alain when she took him in there for their meal.

30

"Something smells delicious," Alain said walking in the front door. Until Jessica came into his life, he hadn't had a home-cooked meal made for him in ages. Not since Melanie's accident. It was either a lot of take-out, Luigi's or his own cooking.

He found Jessica in the kitchen, bent over the counter flipping through a magazine. "Hi gorgeous," he said leaning over and kissing her on the cheek. "I thought seeing how you were making the extra effort, I would, too." He produced a bouquet of long-stemmed, yellow roses and handed them to her. A single yellow bloom in the middle had red tips on the petals.

"Thank you," she exclaimed throwing her arms around him and hugging him. "They're beautiful. Let me put them in water."

"They'll keep for a moment," he replied, his voice husky with desire. He removed the flowers from her grasp and placed them on the counter. Tipping her chin up with his thumb and index finger, he kissed her. "I could take you right here and now on the kitchen table," he whispered. He kissed her again coaxing her mouth open with his tongue.

***

Things weren't going the way Jessica envisioned. Yes, she wanted to make love with Alain. But not in the kitchen with supper in the oven, and not before showing him her afternoon discoveries. She thought about the widow's walk. When she was up there the first time fantasizing about making love to him under the stars.

Using all the tact she could muster, she broke their kiss and stood back. "W-we don't have time right now," she faltered.

"Not even for a quickie?"

"Not even for a quickie," she responded. If she was going to get undressed for sex then she wanted more than an in, out, repeat if necessary. That was too much like her ex. Where on earth had that thought come from?

Jessica glanced at the oven timer. Depending on how long it took Alain to look over the documents, they might not have time to go through the entire coffer. What they didn't see before, they could look at over supper. "Come with me. I want, no I need, you to see this stuff. I promise I'll make it worth your while."

***

Make it worth his while, eh? That was an offer he couldn't turn down. If Jessica was willing, over time they could make love in every room in the house. Give it a proper christening. Alain let her take his hand and lead him into her sitting room. His mind wandered over what she might have in mind for later. He had to stop thinking about it. The more he did, the more he wanted her without delay.

"You need to look at these things," Jessica ordered, showing him the wingback chair. She dragged over the footstool and sat in front of him.

The neck of her sweater was low and loose enough that he could see down her cleavage to her black lace bra. She wasn't helping him curb his desires.

He opened the box and read the newspaper articles and the love letters. "Old Asher was a randy beggar. Keeping two women on the go at the same time," he mused.

"That's not why I wanted you to see these."

"Why then?"

The oven timer went off and she left him bewildered about the importance of these old papers.

***

Jessica pulled the lasagna out of the oven and sat the dish on the top of the stove. It needed to cool a bit before she cut it. She took the salad out of the fridge, cut a lemon into wedges and put them on a plate. Next, she added garlic flavoured croutons to the bowl.

Carrying the dressing and lemon pieces into the dining room, Jessica sat them on the table. She lit the candles before returning to the kitchen for the salad and tongs.

When she returned, she dimmed the lights setting the mood. "You can come through to the dining room, now," she called through the pocket doors.

Minutes later Alain appeared. "Not sure what you've cooked but it smells amazing."

"Nothing special. It's lasagna I made a while ago and froze. I hope it turns out all right. I confess I've not tried freezing my own before."

"It will be fine," he assured.

Jessica poured the dressing over the salad and gave it a quick toss. "Go ahead. Help yourself." She turned and pulled the kitchen door closed.

Taking a sip of her wine, she looked at Alain. "I didn't show you everything. This afternoon when I was looking at the contents of the chest, the crow brought me this. I cleaned it up. I think it's a piece of material from Lucille Walker's clothing. The outfit she wore in the photograph in her missing person article." She slid the fabric to the middle of the table, waiting and watching for his reaction.

"Well there, Mrs. Fletcher, aren't you quite the amateur sleuth?"

Hurt at the comparison to a television character, Jessica gulped down a sob. He wasn't taking her seriously.

"Lucille Walker disappeared over a hundred years ago. It can't be from her."

"You didn't see how filthy it was. Maybe it was buried somewhere all this time and just recently surfaced. Besides, Sherlock, was her disappearance ever solved? Was she found dead or alive?" If he was flippant with her, she was going to give it right back to him.

"I don't know. A body would have to go back through all the old records, and I'm not sure where they would be from back then."

"Well, I think this is a clue." Jessica stood, scooped up the scrap of material, and rushed to the kitchen.

Bracing herself against the counter, she drew in some deep breaths. She put on a pair of oven mitts and carried the lasagna to the dining room.

"I'm sorry," Alain said, his voice sounding sheepish. "I knew this was important to you and I didn't take it or you seriously." He stood and took the casserole dish from her and put it on the trivets. "Jaysus, that's hot," he exclaimed shaking his hands.

"I hope you'll still be able to use them later," she quipped.

Neither spoke during the rest of their meal. Despite being in the same room at the same table, Jessica felt like there was an ocean between them. Alain had taken her excitement and dashed it. He'd stomped it to bits. She doubted Jessica Fletcher ever had a crow bring her gifts. Had he referred to her as Agatha Christie or Miss Marple, she might not be so hurt by his comments. Sure, he was a police officer and looked at things from a different side than she did. Still, he could have shared her enthusiasm.

The longer Jessica sat there, the more frustrated and angry she became. Unable to take it any longer, she threw her napkin on the table, stood, and ran out of the room.

31

For a second, Alain sat at the table stunned. Realizing his serious mistake in judgement, he leapt up from the table and strode to the kitchen. The fridge door stood ajar and he assumed she was on the other side of it. He crept over, slipped his arms around her waist and kissed the side of her neck. "I'm sorry," he whispered. "Am I forgiven for being a jackass?"

"Um …." She turned around and faced him. "If you let me close the door and help me clean up … I might."

The sparkle in her eyes was back. Her lips curved at the corners forming a smile. He had dodged a bullet. He couldn't bear to lose Jessica. Alain leaned down, kissed her on the lips and pulled her close to him. He knew he loved her but hadn't been able to say those words. He wondered if he ever would. He thought she felt the same way about him – at least he hoped she did.

***

Jessica pulled away from him. "It's cold standing here in front of the open fridge." She sidestepped the door and closed it. Maybe she had over-reacted to his comment. All she knew was she couldn't stay mad at him.

Sitting in the sink on the opposite side of the room was the bouquet of roses Alain had brought her. "If you can bring the dirty dishes through, I'm going to tend to the flowers. I should have done it ages ago." She went to the sideboard in the dining room and took out her best crystal vase. Before leaving, she retrieved her brass snuffer and extinguished the candles.

While she trimmed the stems and arranged the roses, Alain worked alongside her. He rinsed the plates and put them in the dishwasher, and covered the lasagna pan with foil. Neither spoke while they completed the chores.

"Why don't we take our wine and go up to the widow's walk. It's a lovely evening and the view is to die for."

Alain didn't reply but retrieved their glasses and the open bottle of wine from the dining room table. "After you, m'lady."

Before leaving the kitchen, Jessica ensured she had locked the outside doors there. She checked the status of the front door, too, prior to joining Alain on the stairs. She stopped at her room and pulled a duvet out of the linen chest. "It might get cold," she said trying to maintain her aura of innocence.

32

Alain gripped the wine glasses by the stems in his right hand and tucked the bottle of wine under his arm. He held the padlock still while Jessica inserted the key and unlocked it. Once open, he slipped it from the hasp and hooked it onto one of his belt loops. Giving the hatch a nudge with his shoulder, he raised it then pushed it open the rest of the way with his free hand.

It was a tight fit but they were both able to stand side by side on the top step. He let her climb out first. If she slipped or tripped or something, he would be there to break her fall.

When Alain stepped onto the platform of the widow's walk, the view amazed him. A wrought iron bistro set painted the same shade of green as the roof and the railings sat in the left front corner. Candles of different heights were on the tabletop. He wondered how and when the collection of furniture got up there. Pity the poor buggers who had to carry it up all those steps and out here.

Jessica spread the duvet out near the back of the roof. Alain set the wine and glasses on the table and walked over to her. He slipped his hand between her legs and ran it along the seam of her jeans. Certain she pushed into his hand, he reached around to undo the button. She slapped his hand away.

"Not yet," she whispered.

This was torture. He'd been ready since before their meal. If he waited much longer, the top of his head would blow off from the pent-up desire. Again, he put both his hands between her legs. He rubbed them back and forth holding his thumbs out, caressing her. He kissed her neck and nibbled her earlobe.

She responded to his touch and leaned back against him. He undid the button on her jeans and opened the zipper. Her breaths became shallow and rapid. Alain turned her around and lowered her onto the blanket.

***

Every place Alain touched her burned with desire. It felt like electrical sparks going off. He lay stretched out beside her. Running his hand up her thigh, he dipped it between her legs before continuing under her lightweight sweater to her breast. Her nipple stood up hard and proud when he touched it with his thumb.

He slid his hand back down her body pausing at the top of her black lace panties. His fingers found their way inside and walked their way down her abdomen. The jeans were too tight for Alain to continue. Jessica pulled them down from her hips just enough for him to work his hand beneath the fabric.

"Ooh," she gasped when he slipped first one finger then another into her.

His thumb caressed her sweet spot in rhythm with the gentle in and out motion of his digits. She moved her hips to meet his inward thrusts. When she reached the brink of release, he stopped.

Alain knelt between her legs and removed her jeans and panties. He leaned forward and slipped her sweater off over her head. He cupped her breast in his hand moving the fabric of her bra away from her nipple. He flicked it with his tongue before kissing, licking and nibbling his way back down her body.

Jessica squirmed at his touch. She clutched the duvet. Hot moist breath puffed on the insides of her thighs. Alain put her legs over his shoulders. His tongue flicked and swirled around her sweet spot and wiggled its way into her slippery, eager sex.

When her moment of release came, she locked her legs around Alain's head. Jessica grabbed the duvet in a vice-like grip. She bit down on her other hand to keep from screaming in ecstasy as she rode wave after wave of climax.

Her legs finally went limp allowing Alain to crawl out from between them. His lips grazed their way up her torso to her breasts and neck. When he reached her mouth, he kissed her. His tongue found hers. She tasted herself on him. At the same time, he thrust his hot, hard member inside. With every stroke, he brushed her sweet spot. She wrapped her legs around him, gripped his firm ass with her hands and sucked on his tongue. Any. Minute. Now. One final time. Alain pushed hard into her. Their orgasms were simultaneous.

They remained in this position, their lips locked together. Their tongues continued exploring each other's mouths. This was even better than the first time they had made love at his apartment.

***

Spent, Alain rolled off. For a few moments, he lay on his back with his arm resting on his forehead. He debated getting dressed – at least his pants. But one look at Jessica, who had shifted so her back was to him, made him change his mind. He spooned her. Wrapped his arm over her and pulled her close protecting her. He kissed the back of her neck.

"Mmm," she whispered. "This didn't work out quite the way I planned. I thought we would drink our wine and watch the sunset first. Not that I'm complaining, mind."

"You're beautiful, Jessica Maitland." He kissed her again. Could he use the *L* word? Could he say love? He swallowed hard. "This isn't going to come out right. But you're the first person I've felt this way about since … since, Melanie died." He paused waiting for a reaction. "I love you." There he said it. It felt like a weight had been lifted from his shoulders. He wanted to stand up and shout it from the rooftop. That wouldn't do his career with the police any good.

"I knew you'd say it sooner or later." Jessica wiggled back tight to him. "I've known you felt this way for quite a while now."

"You have, have you?" Alain propped himself up on his elbow and looked down at her. "And pray tell, how did you know?"

"We women have ways." She smiled.

"I'll give you that." He kissed her bare shoulder.

"And just so you know. You said it just right."

33

The two lay cuddled under the duvet staring up at the sky. “There’s Cassiopeia,” Jessica said pointing. “It’s such a plain constellation for a Queen. It looks like an M.”

“You think it should be more like Hercules over here.” Alain pointed. “Or maybe even Orion, although not much of it is visible. It’s right on the horizon. You might be able to see more if the trees out on the island weren’t there.”

Astronomy wasn’t a subject Jessica knew a lot about. She knew the basic star formations, Big Dipper, Little Dipper, Cassiopeia, and Orion but that was where her knowledge ended.

The sky clouded over. A few spatters of rain landed on the roof. A bolt of lightning hit the water not far from Hillcrest House. The deafening clap of thunder followed immediately. They scrambled for their clothes and scurried down into the stairway. Alain dashed back outside and rescued their glasses and the bottle of wine. Jessica waited below. Despite the fact a bolt of lightning could strike the wet, metal roof and fry him to a crisp, she laughed. He looked so funny running, hunched over so passersby on the street wouldn’t see him in his state of undress. Leastways, that was the only reason she could think of for him to assume that position.

Jessica went on down to the bathroom and placed the armload of clothing on the hamper. She took her housecoat off the hook on the back of the door. Shrugging it on and tying the belt as she went, Jessica entered the walk-in linen closet and dug out towels. When she heard the hatch close, she yelled, “I’m downstairs. I have your clothes and a towel for you. I left the padlock on the ledge.”

She no sooner uttered those words than the repeated thunk

of the device hitting each step echoed through the house.

It took some time but a wet and naked Alain emerged in the doorway at the foot of the attic stairs. He clutched the wine glasses in one hand, the bottle in the other.

Jessica took the objects from him and nodded to the towel she had retrieved for him to use.

Alain dried off then wrapped the towel around his waist. She smiled at his modesty. Not two minutes before, he stood in front of her without a stitch on. Now he'd become shy.

A cold, clammy chill permeated this level of the house making Jessica shiver. A bead of sweat formed at the base of her hairline and escaped past the collar of her robe running down her back. She looked around for the source of the cold thinking a window was open but she saw nothing.

The thunderstorm grew in intensity becoming fiercer by the moment. Rain lashed at the windows. Bolts of lightning streaked across the sky followed by roaring thunder. The lights flickered a few times but stayed on.

Backing up towards her room, Jessica reached inside the door. She took a flashlight out of her nightstand drawer. If the power were to go out, she would at least have this. She flipped the switch but nothing happened. Whacked it against the palm of her hand and tried it again. Still nothing.

"Let's go downstairs while we can still see to get there," Alain suggested coming out of the bathroom dressed.

Jessica nodded. Something compelled her to stay in this spot. She didn't know who or what but the urge to remain in place was overwhelming. A translucent, white orb hovered at the opposite end of the hall. It then disappeared into the bedroom next to hers. The bedroom leading to the secret passage.

34

Alain felt the chill in the house. He dismissed it as getting drenched earlier in the rain and wandering around naked. The change in the weather and the house made of stone didn't help. He entered the dining room, grabbed the candlesticks and lighter. Walking to the only room with a heat source should the power go out, he placed them on the mantle. There was enough wood stacked beside the fireplace to get them through the night but that was about it.

After his previous attempt to get intimate with Jessica in this room, he wasn't sure he wanted to spend time in it. Still, the forensics team had inspected every inch from bottom to top and the gaps between the joists above. They'd found nothing. He laid a fire and soon flames danced and wood crackled on the grate.

When Jessica entered the room, she had changed out of her housecoat into a pair of sweatpants and a baggy hoodie. She wore a pair of slipper booties with pompoms at the sides on her feet. If anyone else came along dressed like that, he wouldn't give him or her a second look. But it was Jessica and she could make a potato sack look sexy.

She turned on the battery-operated candles and placed them on the end tables. "I've got every battery under the sun, except for what I need for my flashlight. Double A, triple A, disc batteries; you name it I have it. But do I have Cs or Ds? No. How could I be so stupid? I always had a flashlight in my nightstand drawer for emergencies. Fat lot of good it does with dead batteries in it."

"Don't be hard on yourself. You've had a lot on your plate since you arrived here in Angel Falls." Alain drew her into his arms and hugged her. She bathed or showered before she came downstairs. He didn't hear the water running but she smelled of vanilla bath and shower gel. "You smell good," he said and kissed her forehead.

"The wine. I forgot to bring it in. I went out to the kitchen to do something and left it on the counter."

"I'll go get it. You stay here."

When Alain entered the kitchen, the curtains in the window over the sink were ablaze. He yanked them down complete with rod, and turned the water on over them extinguishing the flames, singeing the hairs on his arms and hands. His fingers burned from grabbing the ignited fabric. Yet not even a scorch mark showed on the cabinets. Did Jessica start the fire? She'd come out here earlier.

Checking the drawer where she kept her big Maglite, he pulled it out. It didn't turn on. The batteries in it had to be dead. Strange, though. It worked fine when he went to the cellar. The light blinding, it had been so bright. Now? Dead.

He started to leave but remembered he had come in for the wine. Grabbing the glasses and bottle from the counter, he turned the light off with his elbow and left the room. Best not mention this encounter, at least not straight away.

When he returned, Jessica spread a wool blanket on the floor in front of the fireplace. Emblazoned across the seat of her sweat pants in capital letters was the word *naughty*. He smiled to himself when he read it.

A bolt of lightning illuminated the night sky. The deafening thunder cracked and rumbled at the same time. Jessica jumped and yelped. The house plunged into darkness.

The last flash must have hit one of the finials Alain reasoned. The one on the turret was the logical choice since it was the highest point. "I'm going to check everything's okay." He reached for a candle, choosing a battery-operated one since it wouldn't blow out.

"You're not leaving me in here by myself." Jessica took his right hand in her left and clutched his arm with her other one.

With Jessica in tow, he climbed the stairs up to the attic level. Alain wanted to ensure the house wasn't leaking. The sound of the pounding rain on the metal roof sounded like machine gun fire. He didn't hear the splat of water hitting the floor which was a good thing. Candlelight wasn't bright enough to check for wet patches, the precursor to drips. That would have to wait for the sun to come up.

They worked their way down to the second level and inspected it. Everything seemed to be in order. Same with when they reached the first floor. Alain opened the front door and stepped out onto the verandah. Without venturing out into the torrential downpour, everything appeared normal. He walked to the end of the porch in front of the fireplace room and peered around the corner. One of the large maple trees at the back of the property had been split. A huge piece lay on the ground. Maybe the lightning hit it and not the house after all. He checked the other side of the house the same way.

The thunderstorm had moved on. The light show now flashes of white in the sky. The sounds became a distant rumble. Unfortunately, the rain hadn't slowed. At this rate, Angel Falls would be flowing at its peak. He tried to put that thought out of his mind.

When they returned to the house, the fire had dwindled. Alain put another log on and stirred the coals. They would hunker down in here for the rest of the night. He checked his watch. It was now going on three. He had to be back on duty for seven. He wouldn't get much sleep tonight. They sat on the floor with their backs against the sofa. Alain put his arm around Jessica's shoulder and pulled her close.

35

Jessica woke sometime later to heavy pounding on her front door. She staggered to her feet and stumbled into the foyer. Through the sheer curtain, she saw Mr. Bell on the verandah. He had a cut on his forehead and blood oozed from it.

"Mr. Bell, you're bleeding. What happened?" she asked pulling the door open.

"The storm … the storm."

By now, Alain was in the hall at Jessica's side. "Mr. B, are you okay?" he asked.

"The storm … the storm."

"You stay here, Jess. I'll go with him. See if I can make some sense out of this."

"I'm coming, too." She stepped outside. A few small branches littered the front yard. With last night's wind and rain, she wasn't surprised. It was quiet. Too quiet. Not a whisper of traffic noise drifted up the cliff from the main road below the hill. The lack of birdsong, eerie. Had the apocalypse happened?

The three walked out to the wrought iron fence and turned to face the house. Every tree on the property had been felled – broken off or split but they were down. Not one left standing. Another unexpected expense Jessica wasn't prepared for. The only good thing was she would have an ample supply of firewood for the coming season and beyond.

"It was hell and damnation," Mr. Bell finally uttered.

"What do you mean?" Jessica asked.

"The storm. Eunice sent me to check that you're okay."

They continued their surveillance of the damage. Not one of the huge trees hit the house. Alain's car remained unscathed. Hers buried beneath branches. They couldn't assess the damage until after cleanup.

"I've never seen anything like it. Never."

"What's that Mr. B?" Alain asked.

"The storm."

"You've said that," Jessica replied.

"It was the worst I've seen in all the years I've lived at Angel Falls. And the strangest."

"Let's get you inside where I can clean up that cut on your head."

***

"Hurrying to get over here and see you were all right. You know what Eunice can be like."

Jessica nodded. "Go on."

"Well, not paying any attention and walked into a low hanging branch over by the guardrail at the top of the falls. I know it's there. I've ducked under or walked around it umpteen times over the years. Not today. Bang! I walked straight into it."

Wound cleaned and bandage applied, she sat down at the table with the old man.

"You were saying about the storm?"

"Good news, Jess," Alain announced entering the kitchen. "I think your car is all right. It looks like the branches formed a cocoon around it. It'll take some fancy maneuvering to get it and the tree separated."

"Mr. Bell was just about to tell me about the storm."

Alain pulled up a chair and joined them at the table.

"Well, Eunice and me. We were just on our way to bed when it started. We went outside to check on things. Make sure the outbuildings were secure and the like. Lightning like we've never seen. Swirling clouds and all over top of here – your house. No place else. Hell and damnation, I tell you. When that bolt hit the top of the rod on the turret, we watched the fireball follow the wire to the ground. Thought for sure your house was going to burn or blow up or something."

Jessica stood and walked to the window. Her curtains –

burnt and melted – were in the sink. She inspected the cabinets then turned to Alain.

"I was going to tell you but I didn't want to worry you last night … this morning … whenever. When I came out to get the wine, they were on fire. I yanked them down and doused them but good under the tap. Strangest thing though, there was no damage to anything but them."

Chills ran down Jessica's spine. She gripped the countertop to steady herself. A storm happened over her house and nowhere else. A fire in the kitchen causing no destruction other than to a pair of curtains. How? Who? She began to hyperventilate.

Alain grabbed hold of her and got her back onto her chair.

Jessica rested her forehead on the table. Pains shot through her chest and she clutched at it thinking she was having a heart attack.

"Paper bags, have you got any?" Alain snapped.

Waving her arm towards the fridge, she gasped. "Fridge. Mushrooms in crisper."

Mr. Bell leapt out of his chair as if shot from a cannon. Jessica watched him dump the mushrooms out onto the counter. Some rolled onto the floor.

Alain snatched the empty sack. He held it over Jessica's nose and mouth. "Breathe," he commanded.

Once Jessica's breathing returned to normal, the pains in her chest disappeared. "What happened?"

"You had a panic attack. You'll be all right now," Alain said. He picked her up and carried her to the fireplace room and laid her on the couch.

36

Jessica pulled the blanket up over her. She'd never had a panic attack before and it scared the life out of her. She hoped she never had one again. Alain sat by her side and Mr. Bell leaned over the back of the couch.

"You gave us a fright, missie," Bill said.

She tried to sit up but immediately became dizzy.

"I've called in to work. I'm staying here with you," Alain stated.

"You don't have to. I'll be fine."

"Don't argue. It's already done."

"Well I best be getting back home. I'll tell Eunice you're fine but she'll know something's up and be around here faster than you can shake a stick."

Jessica watched Alain see Mr. Bell off from her vantage point on the couch. She tried sitting up but again became lightheaded and woozy. She resigned herself to spending the day napping. Maybe a good sleep would help.

Her slumber was far from restful. Nightmares haunted her. Asher Hargrave falling through the floor at the sawmill. She relived the discovery of her own baby dead in her crib. She saw the Hargrave twins lying lifeless on the beach. A pregnant, faceless woman murdered before her eyes. Maggie Hargrave throwing herself off the roof.

Tossing and turning, Jessica tried to wake up. The more she struggled the more vivid the dreams became. Asher not only fell through the floor, but into the spinning blade. Blood spattered everywhere including all over her.

***

Alain tried waking her but he couldn't. Her arms flailed in the air. Her head shook back and forth. She screamed. Tears ran down her face. He was about to call 9-1-1 when the doorbell rang. Clutching his mobile in his hand, he sprinted to the door.

"Mrs. B. Am I glad to see you. Jess is having a nightmare. I can't wake her up. I was about to call the ambulance."

She pushed past him and into the fireplace room. Kneeling beside the sofa, she grabbed one of Jessica's hands and held it tight.

Alain stood in the doorway with his free hand on the back of his head. Whatever Mrs. Bell was saying and doing helped. Jessica calmed and a few moments later opened her eyes. "Thanks, Mrs. B," he said striding towards them.

"I came to check on you. Yes, I sent Bill but he's as useless as, well you know. Thought I might as well come and see for myself."

"Can I get you a cup of tea or coffee?" Alain offered.

"Is the power back on?" Jessica asked. "I need to check on my computer and other electronic stuff up in my office. After that storm, it's likely all fried." She started to get up from her resting place.

"No, you don't. I'll check. You're not working today anyway. You're taking it easy."

"He's right, dear. You need your rest. Can you remember any of your dream?" Mrs. Bell changed the subject.

"No."

"Just as well. You were in a terrible state. Screaming and flailing. Crying. I've never seen anyone in such a deep but disturbed sleep."

Relief washed over Alain seeing Jessica awake. He walked into the hall and flipped a light switch. The power was back.

He trudged up the stairs to the attic muttering about the location Jessica had chosen for her office. The nursery, preserved as such, would have been a far better choice. The red power indicator on the surge protector was off. It must have tripped. He turned it off and on again but nothing happened. Unplugged it and tried a different outlet. Still nothing. He removed the computer's power cable and plugged it straight into the receptacle. The computer turned on. Whether any of Jessica's software worked was another story. At least she wouldn't have to replace her laptop.

He trotted down the stairs and made a carafe of coffee. "Your computer is fine," he said when he walked into the fireplace room carrying the tray. "Your surge protector not so much. It made the ultimate sacrifice."

Jessica smiled.

Seeing that lifted Alain's spirits but he still worried about her and always would. But, she seemed to be feeling better and that was the important thing.

Mrs. Bell stayed for another hour. They chatted about everything except the storm and Jessica's nightmare. "Well, I best make tracks for home. Bill will be wondering where I've gotten to. Now do you need me to bring you anything for your supper? A casserole?"

Before Alain could reply, Jessica said, "Thanks, but we have leftover lasagna from last night. We can heat it up."

"If you're sure."

"I am. Thank you," Jessica replied.

Alain walked the woman to the front door. "I don't know how to thank you, Mrs. B. I don't mind saying so but Jess scared the hell out of me. I've never seen anything like it before and I definitely don't want to ever again."

"I'm happy I was able to help. You two make a lovely couple. I'm glad you finally got together. Bye." Eunice smiled, turned and walked down the path to the front gate.

How did she know that he and Jess were a couple? He closed the front door, pondering the question. He concluded Jessica told her while he was checking on the power and the state of the computer. He smiled.

37

The next morning, Jessica woke early. She felt refreshed. Alain lay alongside with his back to her. Slipping out of bed quietly so she didn't wake him, she put her slippers on, grabbed her robe off the hook on the door and padded down to the kitchen.

She started the Keurig and brewed herself a cup. Set it to brew strong. After the day before, she needed the extra caffeine jolt. Relieved that her computer still worked, she only had to replace the power bar; Jessica started a shopping list for the next time she went to the city.

Today she was going to get the first coat of paint on in the last bedroom. This was the one over the fireplace room. The one that the secret passage opened into and always felt cold and clammy inside even though the radiator pumped out the heat. She might even get more than one applied depending on how well it went on.

Jessica turned on the radio, keeping the volume down since Alain was still asleep. She danced around the kitchen humming along with the music. When she saw him leaning on the doorframe with his arms folded across his chest, she stopped dead. "I'm sorry. I didn't mean to wake you."

"You didn't. I was already awake." He strode towards her. "Are you going to be okay here today? After yesterday, I hate to leave you." He enveloped her in his arms and kissed her neck.

"I'll be fine. Don't worry." She wriggled out of his grip. As much as Jessica wanted Alain to stay, she knew he had to go back to work. He'd taken the previous day off because of her and she wasn't going to let him take more. "Do you want a coffee before you leave? Machine's hot."

"I'll pass. I still have to get back to my place, shower and get into uniform." He kissed her again. "I'll call you later. See how you're doing. Love you."

"I love you, too." Jessica unlocked the side kitchen door so he could go out that way. She watched him get into his car and drive off, waving to him until he was well out of sight.

When she first moved to Angel Falls, she didn't plan on a new relationship. She was still coming to terms with the breakup of her marriage. But Alain was the right tonic for her. She smiled picturing his handsome face.

***

Jessica changed into her painting clothes and gathered the necessary supplies for the job. She assembled them in the hall outside the bedroom. "Okay, Asher. Do your worst. I'm coming in," she announced.

Turning the knob, she pushed the door open. The clammy cold air from within rushed into the corridor. Jessica shivered but continued into the room. That same foul odour that drove her and Alain out of the house after the wine and cheese party wafted in the air. It wasn't strong like before. She likened it to the smell of skunk in the distance. Stinky enough to know it was there but not to the point where it was sickening. The radiator was warm to the touch but not hot. She turned the heat up. Once she was working, she could turn it down again. Right now, she wanted to take the chill off.

Jessica prepared the first wall for painting. She worked towards the end of the room where the secret passage opened. Because of the high ceilings, she needed a ladder and still had to use an extension on the roller handle. It took about an hour and a half to get a single coat on the one surface.

Sweating now, Jessica turned the heat back to its original setting. She debated opening the secret passage from the other side before she painted. In the end, she decided against it. The wardrobe would be in front of it so no one would ever see any imperfections.

The front wall with its windows was time consuming to

complete. Even though there wasn't the same amount of surface needing colour, it took longer to paint. She wiped the perspiration from her forehead with the back of her hand. Jessica reached for the water bottle on the nightstand and took a healthy swig.

Before she could tackle the last wall in the room, she had to move the furniture. At least the bedside tables weren't too heavy and moved with ease across the floor. The bed, that was another story. Jessica pushed on the footboard but it didn't budge. She came up to the headboard and tried there. Still no luck. It was like the bed had been in the same position and never moved since the Hargraves lived here. She tried lifting the side by the rail. It was too heavy. Frustrated, Jessica kicked it dislodging it from its stuck position. She managed to move it over and out from the wall.

When she stepped across the floor, a couple of the boards felt loose under her feet. She dropped to her knees and felt the area where she'd just stepped. The planks floated in the space between the others.

Jessica grabbed the large straight screwdriver she used to open the paint can. She pushed the blade between the slats on the floor. One end lifted but not high enough to get her fingers under it. She needed more leverage. The stick she used to stir the latex.

On her next attempt, she lifted the end of the floorboard, shoved the stick under the side. Trying to raise the board higher, she twisted the piece of wood. It worked. Jessica got her hand under the board and tipped it away from her.

Rocking back on her heels, she rubbed her palms on her thighs. She took a deep breath and peered into the cavity. Something was in there. Jessica reached in. Her fingers wrapped around an object. She pulled her hand out. She held a bone! "Oh my God," she screamed into the empty house.

38

If there was one, there had to be more. Jessica fumbled in her pockets to find her phone. It had a flashlight feature on it. She'd never used it before but scrolled through the icons until she found it.

She shoved the board she'd removed off the adjacent one and lifted it out of the way. Holding her mobile so that the light shone into the opening, she made a gruesome discovery. The skeletal remains of not one but two bodies – human bodies concealed in the space for who knows how long.

Despite the hideous find, she couldn't tear herself away from the sight. With the position of the bones, it appeared to be a mother and her unborn child. Had Jessica found the remains of Lucille Walker and her baby?

This find excited her. She had to call the police. She took pictures with her phone so she could text them to Alain. He would know what she needed to do next. She typed *U need 2 see this. Found under floor. Tell me what 2 do* into her message and attached the pictures. Her finger hovered over the send button for a few seconds before she hit it.

Her phone rang startling her. "Alain?"

"I got your text. You need to get out of the house – now. It's a crime scene. Forensics are on their way."

"But …," she protested.

"You have to do this. I'll be along as soon as I can."

Sirens wailed in the distance. Jessica knew they were coming to Hillcrest House. She refused to leave. If these were the remains of Lucille Walker and her unborn child, she was going to do her best to protect them now. No one had done so before.

Watching the black SUV pull around the corner onto

Richard Street, she knew it wouldn't be long until the police would be at her door demanding entry.

Jessica slunk away from the window. She walked to the only wall she hadn't painted yet and slid down until she sat on the floor. She drew her knees to her chest and wrapped her arms around her legs.

Thunderous pounding on the front door shook the house. "Police. Open up," a gruff voice yelled.

Burying her face and resting her forehead on her knees, Jessica cried.

***

Alain pulled his Crown Victoria to a stop on the wrong side of the street on Royal Avenue. He turned on the flashing lights and climbed out.

"That crazy bitch won't let us in," Gus complained.

"Watch your mouth. That crazy bitch as you call her is my girlfriend."

"You're getting laid then. About fucking time," Jake quipped. "Maybe you won't be such a sore ass all the time now."

"I'm going to pretend I didn't hear that. Give me a couple of minutes with her, okay?" Alain pulled a key out of his pocket and unlocked the front door. "A couple of minutes," he repeated shooting them a warning look. He opened the door wide enough to slip in and locked it behind him before they had a chance to follow.

Taking the stairs two at a time, it didn't take long to reach the bedroom where he found Jessica. He crept in and sat on the floor beside her. "You okay?" he whispered.

She nodded.

"The guys have to come in. They have work to do." He murmured not wanting to scare her and create more problems.

"I can't leave them."

"Yes, you can." Alain put his arm around her shoulder and pulled her to him. "You have to."

She shook her head.

"Come on, Jess. We need to get out of here and let the guys do what they do best." Alain stood and held his hand out to her.

Looking up at him through tear-streaked eyes, she took his hand. He helped her to her feet.

"I'll leave the room but not the house."

"What?" He thought he'd gotten her to agree to leaving.

"I'll stay out here out of the way. I can't go. They need me."

Ready to bang his head against the wall, Alain rolled his eyes. Why did she have to be so stubborn? He had to strike a compromise with the forensics team. He sat her on the bottom step leading to the attic and went down to let Gus and Jake in. "She refuses to leave the house but she did agree to leave the room. She found some old love letters in a wooden chest here a while ago. Love letters between Asher Hargrave and the domestic, Lucille Walker. She disappeared when she was pregnant back in the early 1900s."

"And your girlfriend here thinks it's her duty to protect the bones," Gus moaned.

"You got yourself one nutcase there, Fournier."

"Watch your mouth, Jake."

The men pulled on their white boiler suits and entered the house. Once over the threshold, they donned the blue paper booties. Alain led them to the room where Jessica had made the discovery then sat with her on the attic stairs.

***

Bursts of bright light flashed around the edges of the closed bedroom door. Jessica knew the forensics team was photographing the room, the bones, the space between the floor joists and who knew what else. She stood and paced back and forth in the corridor.

"Come sit down," Alain urged standing with his hands on her shoulders. "This isn't going to speed the work up. It will take as long as it takes."

Jessica shook him off and continued her sentry duty from

one end of the hall to the other chewing on her thumbnail. If the bones were those of Lucille and her unborn baby, who killed them? Did Maggie? In the one letter from Lucille to Asher, she mentioned Mrs. Hargrave boarded the train. Had she forced Lucille back here only to murder her? Or did she entice her back with lies? Tell the poor frightened young woman that despite the affair, she still loved her husband? And since it was his child Lucille carried, they would raise it here at Hillcrest House? Scenario after scenario flashed through her mind.

When she walked by the door to the bedroom, Jessica heard one of the men's voices but she couldn't make out his words. The investigation seemed to last forever.

"That's us away," Jake said sitting his bag on the floor.

Gus exited next carrying a box. Once he was out, Jake closed the door and sealed it with crime scene tape. The two diagonal strips formed a huge X across it.

"B-but my paint," Jessica stammered. "I can't leave the can open in there for who knows how long. It will dry out."

"I put the lid back on the can – tight. You'll lose what's in the tray and most likely your brush and roller," Jake said.

"So what happens next?" she asked.

"We take the bones to the morgue and then a forensic anthropologist goes to work," Jake explained.

"How long will it all take?"

"Six months, maybe a year," Gus said, taking the cardboard box downstairs.

Dejected, Jessica flopped onto one of the lower stairs to the attic. Life at Hillcrest House hadn't been normal since she moved in. Now it could be more of the same for up to twelve months. Maybe even longer.

39

"Come on downstairs, Jess," Alain urged. "There's nothing more you can do." He helped her up, put his arm around her shoulders and escorted her to the main level.

He knew the remainder of the investigation would take as long as it took to identify the bones, determine their age, sex. Being a cold case, it wouldn't receive the same priority as a current one. The television programs that wrapped everything up in an hour made it difficult for people to understand that in reality, these things took much longer.

Alain left Jessica in the kitchen and went outside to talk to the team who were loading the evidence into the SUV. "Any thoughts?" he asked.

"Other than what we found under the floor is too old to have caused the black putrefaction we investigated on our first call out here?"

That night was the last thing Alain wanted to remember. It ended well back at his apartment but it didn't start out that way. He scrubbed his hand over his head. "Yeah," he replied.

"Sorry pal. You're going to have to wait for the results just like …" Jake nodded towards the kitchen door. "Like your lady friend there."

***

"You lock up," Jessica cried, dashing by Alain and the forensics team. Tears filled her eyes blurring her vision. She ran until she thought her lungs would explode. Stopping to catch her breath, she bent over with her hands on her thighs. Her chest heaved as she gulped in air.

She didn't know how far she'd run since she left Hillcrest

House. When Jessica straightened up, she found herself outside Cliffside Guest House. Since she'd come this far, she thought she would check on Mr. Bell and see how he was after his encounter with the tree branch.

Jessica rang the doorbell. While she waited for someone to answer it, she bent down and untied her paint splattered running shoes.

"Oh, it's you, Jessica. Come in, dear. Come in," Eunice greeted when she opened the door.

"Thought I'd see how Mr. Bell is doing." Jessica took off her trainers revealing a pair of sport socks covered in neon pink, orange and cyan stripes.

"You have the cutest socks," Mrs. Bell commented.

Rubbing one foot against her calf, Jessica smiled and her cheeks flushed.

"You just missed Bill. He's gone for his newspaper. Come, we'll have a chat over coffee."

"I suppose I'm the talk of the town again after the storm and now having the police there again."

"Everyone knows you and Alain are an item. Why would they think it strange if he's there with his cruiser?"

"Not just him," Jessica said pulling out a chair. "The forensics team is there. Well, they were there. When I moved the bed to paint the wall over the fireplace room, a couple floorboards were loose. I pulled them up and found a skeleton."

Mrs. Bell dropped the mug she'd taken out of the cupboard. She juggled it and caught it before it hit the floor. "Really?" She joined Jessica at the table.

"Actually, it was two skeletons. I think I found the remains of Lucille Walker and her unborn baby." Before Mrs. Bell could react to this latest bit of news, Jessica related her discovery of the love letters between the maid and Asher Hargrave – the newspaper account of the woman's disappearance, and the crow bringing the scrap of material matching the outfit Lucille wore in the photo accompanying her missing person article.

"Things have certainly been eventful since you arrived at Hillcrest House. Now let's have that coffee."

Not knowing how to broach the subject, when Eunice returned with the tray, Jessica decided to just come out and ask. "The first time we talked, you said Hillcrest House used to be such a pretty place. How did you know?"

"I knew it would only be a matter of time before you asked," Mrs. Bell sighed and left the room. When she returned, she placed an aged photo album on the table in front of Jessica. "Go ahead, dear. Open it," she urged as she sat back down.

Nodding, Jessica opened the book. Old black and white pictures, held in place with silver photo corners, surrounded a larger one of Hillcrest House. With the weight of the paper, she guessed the picture dated back to the early 1900s.

With care, she moved on to the next page and the one after that. When she had been through the entire album, Jessica started again at the beginning. "How did you get all these pictures?"

"Well, my great-grandmother was Maggie Hargrave's sister."

"You're related to the Hargraves?"

"Only through Maggie's marriage. She and her sister were Roberts." Mrs. Bell came around the table and stood at Jessica's shoulder. She flipped through the pages and stopped at a picture of a group of adults and children on a picnic. "This was Elizabeth, my great-grandmother," she said pointing. "There's Maggie and Asher and their children, Charles, Elizabeth (named after my great-grandmother), and little Maggie. This other girl is my grandmother Ophelia. I'm not sure who the last one is."

Jessica leaned closer. "It's Lucille. When they took this picture, she'd be a teenager. I know she worked for the Hargraves but it looks like they treated her like one of their own. But why, when you can see everyone else's feet, can't you see hers? It's like she's hiding something."

"I don't like to speak ill of the dead, but family folklore says she had six toes on each foot. Supposedly, a hereditary condition."

Squirming, Jessica tucked her toes behind the legs of her chair. "I-If your great-grandmother and Maggie were sisters, why didn't she inherit the house after Maggie's death?"

"The house belonged to the Hargrave family long before Asher and Maggie married. It went to Asher's brother, Charles."

Trying to keep track of all the names proved difficult when parents named their children after aunts and uncles. While the pictures shed light on the Hargrave family dynamics and lineage, they did nothing to reveal Lucille's secrets. Secrets that she took to the grave with her.

"Thanks for the coffee, Mrs. Bell. Sorry I missed Bill. Please tell him I stopped in." Jessica stood and hurried out of the house. Learning of Lucille's birth defect made her uncomfortable. She grabbed her shoes and struggled into them on the step before returning home.

40

When Jessica got back to Hillcrest House, Alain and the forensics team were gone. She patted her pockets for her keys. They weren't there. She'd left them inside when she rushed out earlier.

The branches on the fallen tree still surrounded her small car. She'd have to get someone in to cut the wood. Jessica found an opening big enough to get her arm through up to her shoulder so she could reach inside the wheel well and retrieve the magnetic key case. She'd never kept an extra car key in it but stashed one for the house, instead. Not that she thought anyone would steal her Aveo but she wasn't about to give them carte blanche by leaving a key to the vehicle there.

Jessica let herself in through the door at the back of the kitchen. After she tossed the key onto the counter, she opened the fridge and grabbed a bottle of water. She had to do some research. Mrs. Bell answered some of her questions but, still more remained.

Climbing the steps to the turret, Jessica formulated a plan of what she'd look for and the order she'd do it in. She turned her computer on. While she waited for it to boot, she took a swig of water. A google search revealed nothing on Lucille Walker, at least not *her* Lucille Walker. She looked up six toes. The images on the results screen piqued her interest so she clicked on the link. Some of the photos were revolting but she couldn't look away. Mrs. Bell had mentioned Lucille's condition being hereditary. Jessica wondered from which side of the girl's family it came.

Since Jessica turned nothing fruitful up so far, she decided to try ancestry. The worst that would happen is she wouldn't find anything. Without signing up with a credit card for a two-week free trial, something she didn't want to do, her efforts were stymied.

Lucille had gone to the nuns for help. Jessica googled convents near Angel Falls. The Good Sisters of Mercy once had one in nearby Queenston in the old part of the city. The place, while no longer home to the religious order, housed a museum. Jessica wondered if this was where the frightened and pregnant Lucille turned in her time of need – not once but twice.

When she uncovered the human remains in the floor, a smaller skeleton lay in the space between the ribs and pelvis. All that proved, if it was Lucille and her unborn child, was that she came back to Hillcrest House only to become a murder victim. In the last letter Lucille wrote to Asher, she mentioned her rape and her parents sending her to the convent to live. She managed to drag it out of the nuns that she'd given birth to a daughter.

Jessica looked down at her feet. No, it wasn't possible was it? She reached for her phone to call her mother then remembered she had died of ovarian cancer the previous year. Those memories flooded back and her eyes filled with tears. The odious disease had taken this once vibrant woman and reduced her to skin and bones before her organs shut down and she slipped away.

Her father didn't deal well with his wife's death. He wanted everything of hers removed from the house right away and threatened to burn it, if his wishes weren't carried out. Losing her mother was bad enough but dealing with this on top of her own grief made it unbearable. Jessica donated the clothing to charity. She kept her mother's jewellery, books, photographs and personal papers. Could she find a clue there?

Scrambling into the cubbyhole under the rafters in the attic, Jessica dragged out a huge cardboard box filled with photo albums and envelopes containing who knew what. Organizing this array of paperwork had been a long overdue task but one she couldn't bring herself to tackle. Now, the question was where to start.

Jessica decided to sort by family name. It took about four

hours to get everything into order. She could have done it in less time, but found herself caught up in reading entire documents, not just dates.

Some of the papers dated back as far as 1892 and her great-great grandfather's long-form birth certificate. His marriage registration in 1913 to Georgianna Smith. Nothing tying her to Lucille Walker here. Jessica didn't know what she expected to find, if anything. She continued searching.

Smith. Smith. She had a stack of papers for Smith. Where did she put it? Jessica got on her hands and knees over the piles. She found the one she wanted. Her feet and legs hurt from sitting on the floor so she took the bundle to her drafting table and spread them out.

September 30, 1895

My dear Barbara,

Your letter of August 31 has pleased your father and me immensely. We are thrilled to know of your happiness and are glad you were able to adopt a healthy and happy wee girl. But six toes? I've never heard of such a thing happening with children.

We can't wait to see you and your family and hope you'll come visit us soon. It's far too long between visits.

Love to you and your family,

Mother

Could it be? Was Georgianna Smith Lucille Walker's

illegitimate child from her rape as a teenager? She rifled through the papers. When she found the adoption one, Jessica leaned back on her stool. The document, typed on the Good Sisters of Mercy letterhead and stamped with their seal, listed the parents as George Smith and his wife Barbara. The child, an infant, appeared on the paper as Baby Girl Walker, born August 30, 1895. Visible congenital malformation – six toes on each foot, otherwise the child appeared to be healthy.

Jessica stared at the adoption paper in disbelief. She was a direct descendant of Lucille Walker.

The sound of heavy footsteps on the stairs got louder. "Jess, where are you?" Alain hollered.

When she heard his voice, Jessica breathed a sigh of relief. She was positive she locked the door behind her when she came home from Cliffside Guest House forgetting she'd given Alain a key. "I'm up in my office," she called.

She met him at the top of the stairs and threw her arms around him. "Hey whoa. Let me get into the room if you don't mind," he exclaimed. "I don't want to fall backwards down those." Alain nodded to the steps.

"I missed you. I've had the most fantastic time since the discovery of the bones. Mrs. Bell is related to Maggie Hargrave. I'm a descendant of Lucille Walker," she babbled.

"Slow down. You're not making any sense."

"Come here," she said. Jessica took his hand and dragged him to her drafting table. "Look, this is the adoption paper for Lucille's illegitimate daughter." She thrust the paper in his face. "Eunice's great-grandmother was Maggie Hargrave's sister. She has family pictures and one has Lucille in it. She's standing behind a rock like she's trying to hide something."

Alain laid the document on the table. He wrapped Jessica in his arms and kissed the top of her head. "I saw Jake and Gus before I left the station. They told me with the position of the bones, the deceased was definitely pregnant and birth would most likely have taken place within a few weeks."

Jessica sighed. Someone finally believed her.

"They said it was the damnedest thing. The adult skeleton had six toes on each foot. Now don't go getting all excited yet.

Nothing's proven. It's still all conjecture. Until the forensic anthropologist does his thing we won't know anything for sure."

"I think we do," Jessica whispered. She backed away from Alain, removed her socks, and wiggled her toes – all six on each foot. "It's a hereditary condition," she explained.

"Well I'll be." Alain pulled her close and held her in his arms. He kissed the top of her head and said, "You may have solved a cold case, Mrs. Fletcher."

Also by Melanie Robertson-King

A Shadow in the Past
(4RV Publishing)

The Consequences Collection
Tim's Magic Christmas
(King Park Press)

Cole's Notes (A Short Story)
EFD1: Starship Goodwords – a cross genre anthology
(Carrick Publishing, 2012)

MELANIE ROBERTSON-KING

http://www.melanierobertson-king.com

Melanie Robertson-King has always been a fan of the written word. Growing up as an only child, her face was almost always buried in a book from the time she could read. Her father was one of the thousands of Home Children sent to Canada through the auspices of The Orphan Homes of Scotland, and she has been fortunate to be able to visit her father's homeland many times and even met the Princess Royal (Princess Anne) at the orphanage where he was raised.